SMOKE INTO FLAME

by

JANE ARBOR

D0645280

Harlequin Books

TORONTO • LONDON • NEW YORK • AMSTERDAM • SYDNEY • WINNIPEG

Original hard cover edition published in 1975
by Mills & Boon Limited

SBN 373-01963-7

Harlequin edition published April 1976

Printed in Canada

CHAPTER ONE

AGAINST the blackness of the night the rain appeared like silver rods, coming out of nowhere to crash and break up in fountains of spray, puddling the saturated macadam of the roadway. The road itself stretched darkly ahead and behind as if to infinity in each direction. Its verges had no benefit of street lights, nor neighbourhood houses, nor sheltering trees. Its bordering terrain was bleak and flat, and to Clare, her every breath coming as a half-sob, it had no purpose but that of blind escape.

Ten minutes ago, coming out on it at a stumbling run, she had used no choice in the way she took. Either could serve to put distance between her and the sordid threat of the scene she had quitted. The man, Florio Marciano, had a car; he had brought her there, *tricked* her there, in it, and he might decide to follow her. So then nothing had mattered but to get away, anywhere away as far and as fast as possible. But now, her feet squelching in her evening sandals, soaked through to her skin beneath the thin silk of her dress and light wrap, she halted. This would not do – this blind running. If he had meant to follow her, he must have caught up with her by now, and somehow she judged, now that she was more collected, that he would be too indifferent to do so. As he had sullenly claimed, he had done as he had been asked, had played his part, and she thought she probably had no more to fear from him. Therefore now she must take a hold on herself; decide, if she could, where she was heading; find shelter, a telephone, transport. But how and where did she begin?

Somewhere to seaward lay the city of Rimini. But which way from here was seaward? Completely disorientated by the blanketing rain and the overcast night, she could not tell which point of the compass she faced, and for the same reason she could not hope that the reflected glow of the city's lights could penetrate this gloom.

Nevertheless she looked for them. In vain. She was utterly lost. After a pleasantly innocuous evening – dinner and a floor-show at a restaurant – Florio Marciano had fetched his parked car and had rejoined her to drive her home. They had chatted on the way, and though it had occurred to her fleetingly that the return journey was taking longer than the outward one, she had put this down to the exigencies of one-way and no-entry streets. Until – !

At the memory she shivered and shook her head, and then shivered again, this time with physical penetrating chill. She *must* keep going. The road ran so arrow-straight; it must lead somewhere, however many kilometres ahead. And the rain must stop some time, she supposed.

As she trudged on, the occasional late-travelling car swished past her, showering her with the up-flung muddy spray from its wheels. But instinct warned her against flagging any of them down. One nasty experience in one evening was enough, and in case any driver who stopped for her might be a lone man, she wasn't inviting another. Besides, though her Italian had improved during her three months in Italy, she doubted its adequacy to explain or to justify her present predicament to anyone; indeed she could hardly believe in it herself.

It had all begun so innocently ... First of all, with Giulia Cavour's pleading a bad migraine which would prevent her going out with Florio, her fiancé, that evening, and as he had booked a table and would be very disappointed, her plea to Clare to take her place.

Clare had demurred. Florio would surely be only too willing to cancel the table and take Giulia out another night. Besides, she doubted whether Bruno would care for her going out with another man, even Florio, when he couldn't take her – both of which objections Giulia had dismissed with finality. When she was married to Florio and Clare was married to Bruno they would all be *cognati*, kindred with each other, wouldn't they? So that to dine out with Florio would be for Clare no more than dining with a brother, which Bruno could not fail to understand, and as it was a fiesta night at the restaurant, it would be little short of meanness on Clare's part to disappoint Florio at such short notice. Clare could surely not refuse?

Clare had agreed, though with reluctance, that she could not. Giulia had duly retired to bed behind closed shutters, saying that Mama would get her anything she needed, and when Florio had called in the evening, Clare had changed and was ready to go with him. After all, Bruno, having to work in the evening himself, couldn't mind her having a rare evening out, and no one's behaviour could have been more correct than Florio's, up to the point where they had arrived at that – that *sleazy* motel off the highroad, and he had told her of his orders to keep her there all night.

"*Orders?* Whose?" she had demanded, incensed.

"Giulia's, of course," he had said.

"Giulia told you to – to compromise me like that? Impossible!" she had scoffed.

"Not so at all."

"But I don't understand! *Why?*"

At that he had leered unpleasantly. "Can't you guess? Giulia doesn't like you. Mama Cavour doesn't want you around. Papa Cavour – pouf! He is a nothing, a nobody in the family, and against that set-up Bruno is finding you a bit of a

7

liability, a nuisance. Else why hasn't he put his ring on your finger before now, tell me that?"

"It's none of your business!"

Florio shrugged and spread his hands. "Maybe not. But maybe too Giulia knows what she is about. That she wouldn't be the only one to be glad to see the back of you, I mean. And therefore, once you've spent the night with me, Bruno, as a man of honour, can get out of anything he owes you with dignity. *As*, we have all suspected, he has been wanting to, for some time. An innocent English girl, brought out to meet and get to know his family before marriage – yes. But a light-o'-love who didn't need to be pressed – that's different altogether – yes?"

For that she had hit him – her open palm coming into hard contact with his cheek. And as she had turned to run his grumble had followed her – "And you needn't think I'm interested either. For Giulia I'd do most things – short of making up to a skinny washed-out *inglese* for a whole night. Anyway, after that I'm done with you, you little she-cat. Run, if you must. I couldn't care less where, and I'm telling Giulia she can – "

The rest of his threat had been lost to Clare as she ran. Giulia or no Giulia in command, he hadn't tried to keep her, and now, thinking back, she saw why.

He knew – as she did only too well – that by revealing the miserable plot to her he had accomplished his mission without using force. Now, if that was what they wanted, the Cavours, all of them, were rid of her. She would never face any of them again – not even Bruno, whom she had trusted and of whom she had hoped so much.

Now she remembered. Back in England the too-clever cynics had warned her, "Marry an Italian, and you marry the family, no less." And she, lonely and with no family at all to her name, hadn't listened, hadn't wanted to – then. Of the

8

Cavours, Bruno had told her, there were his mother and father and sister Giulia, and on the side, innumerable aunts and uncles and cousins, all panting to know her and love her, as she, in her turn, was longing to learn to love them.

So she had come out with him to Rimini, and only slowly and even more reluctantly had begun to admit that the clever ones might have got their cynicism right.

For once back in the bosom of his family, Bruno had been absorbed in it, smothered by it, obedient to his dominant mother's every dictate, petty or otherwise, and too often designed to divide him from Clare and to belittle her in his eyes.

Occasionally he would rebel and they would be happy together. But too often and lately almost always, he had given in and taken sides against Clare. And gradually – which was why she had been able to believe Florio – she had had to watch his will to marry her slip away under pressure. Subtly but inexorably, his family was parting them, and though she didn't credit for a moment that Bruno had been in the know of Giulia's plot, she suspected with Florio that he might welcome its results as an excuse to wave her goodbye.

Well, he wasn't going to have the chance. *She* would do any waving there was to be done. To his family too. *Family !* So much for the warmth and welcome and security she had expected from Bruno's. Instead it had proved a juggernaut, mowing its members down – or, if less dramatically, at least moulding them, managing them, forming them to its will. Dejected, lost and abandoned as she was at the moment, her head went up proudly, in defiance of "family" – an ideal she had cherished and which had let her down. When she married – *if* she married after this bitter experience, she would choose a man who hadn't one; as unbeholden to family ties as she was herself. When – if – the time came for her to fall in love and need a man again, she would want to know he was uncluttered, free, hers alone –

Her upward jerk of her head and a rising wind which might or might not drive the rain away, had flung a heavy strand of wet hair across her face. She thrust it back, wringing a stream of water from it as she did so, slinging down her shoulder-bag in search of a handkerchief with which to wipe her wet hands. Standing so, head down, fumbling, she was first aware of the overtaking and then slowing car by the reflection of its head-lights on the shining wetness of the road. She looked up.

At the touch of a button the window slid down and the driver leaned out to her. "*Posso aiutarla, signora ?*" he asked.

This was a situation she hadn't wanted – the possible offer of a lift by a man. But as she stepped back and said, "*No, grazie,*" the flick of another switch brought on the courtesy light and she saw that a young woman was in the back seat. She was looking at Clare with curiosity, as was the driver, as if in disbelief of her refusal of his offer to help her. After an aside to his companion, he said something to Clare which she did not understand. To which, her own Italian deserting her for the moment, she said a little helplessly, "I am English."

The man's dark eyebrows came down. "Ah, English," he said, and went on easily in that language, "I was asking whether your car had broken down and you were on your way in search of a garage or a telephone, perhaps?"

Clare shook her head. "I have no car. I was just – walking," she said.

"*Walking ?* By choice – in this weather?"

"Yes. No. That is – " She nodded ahead. "Does this road lead into Rimini?"

"At two or three kilometres' distance, yes. What part of Rimini do you want?"

She didn't know. Certainly she wasn't returning to the Cavours' tonight. "I'm not sure. I just wanted a hotel – any small hotel for the night," she told her questioner.

"And you prefer to go in search of one in the rain, instead of allowing us to see you into the city, on our way up to San Marino where we live?"

She hesitated, realizing how ungracious her refusal must have sounded. Absurd too. In view of the dreadful night, her bedraggled state, her ignorance of her whereabouts or where precisely she wanted to go, no wonder she could read from his expression that he thought she was crazy! In an effort to back-pedal on her refusal, she began, "You are very kind" – at which the other girl sat forward and urged her, "Come, please. It is no trouble to us. Get in beside my brother. You are so very wet!"

Clare obeyed. As the door closed on her the man introduced himself, "Tarquin Roscuro," and the girl, "My sister, Signora Bernini," in return for which Clare murmured her own name, "Clare Yorke."

She expected further questioning about her plight, but the few remarks which passed were in Italian between the other two, giving her the opportunity to study Signora Bernini's reflection in the driving-mirror.

She had a pleasant round face, incurving dark short hair, and eyes which had the makings of laughter-lines at their corners. She appeared to be in her middle twenties, relaxed and oddly serene beyond her years.

Clare stole a look at the profile beside her, seeking some likeness between brother and sister. There was little, she decided. The man seemed more dynamic, with an erect pride which was all his own. His skin and hair – the latter brushed back into a curve at the nape of his neck – were both darker still than his sister's. Where her features were plump and smooth, his chin, jaw and aquiline nose were strongly sculptured, the lift of his brows – as Clare had already noticed – sharply expressive. It was a face and bearing which she thought she would remember for a long time after she had seen the last of him, which must be quite soon now.

The car passed through the outskirts of the city into the brightly lighted streets of its night life. There Tarquin Roscuro stopped outside the awninged portico of a hotel flashing its name in ornate neons, "Hotel Bellini" – on, off, on, off.

"You are looking for something more modest than this?" he asked.

Clare barely suppressed a shudder. He had chosen the very place where Bruno Cavour was a musician in the hotel orchestra, and at any time now, well after midnight, he might be leaving to go home. "Oh yes, much more. Just a quiet place or a *pensione*," she told her companion, who said with a significant glance at her dampness, "I thought so, but I didn't know what your standards were."

He drove on, while Clare contemplated the dilemma she was in.

Expecting she was only going out for the evening, naturally she had not brought her passport and had in her bag only the small change of about a thousand lire. Some hotels demanded the passports of foreigners, and all of them would expect to be paid! And then the driver spoke over his shoulder to his sister, and Clare caught the phrase, "*Non ha bagaglio*", she faced another difficulty – the fact that she had no luggage, and hotels expected genuine clients to have some. The other two went on talking until the man turned to her to say, "My sister agrees with me that you need to change into some dry clothes, and as, having no luggage with you, you may not be welcomed at this late hour, even at a *pensione*, it might be better if we took you home with us for the night – to the Casa Torre in San Marino. I can drive you back to Rimini in the morning. What do you say? Do you agree to come?"

Did she agree! Only too gratefully, Clare accepted, wondering at their offer of hospitality to this forlorn stranger, but instinctively sure that she, on her side, could trust them. She murmured her thanks in Italian to them both, then prepared to enjoy the lengthened drive.

She had been up to the mountain fastness which was the tiny Republic of San Marino once before with Bruno. That had been in the season of high summer, when the narrow climbing streets had been a'block with tourists and the air a clamour of a dozen different languages as people jostled at souvenir shops and stalls and cafés, or climbed in panting droves, seeking from one of its famous cliff-set towers the fantastic view of the coastline and the plains of Romagna far below.

But now it was early autumn and night time. Even by day the crowds would be less, and by night San Marino came into its own as a fairyland pinnacle, its slopes necklaced by the lights of its winding approach roads – round and round and up and up – towards the deeply crenellated walls which made of the Republic's name-town a fortress which had proved impregnable to hostility for centuries.

The car climbed smoothly, its power making little of the heights it was achieving so gradually. At the Dogana, the Customs post, it was saluted without being stopped. It passed through a gateway into a square, one corner of which was the site of a tall granite house, dark now above its ground-floor façade, which was in deep shadow under a pillared colonnade roofed with pantiles, running the whole length of the frontage.

Here the car drew up and Signora Bernini led the way into a marble-paved hall, lighted by standard lanterns, from which marble stairs, balustrated with wrought iron, went up. She said to her brother, "I shall not disturb Anna. As you say, Signora Yorke can have the tower room." She turned to Clare. "You have dined, *signora*?"

"Oh yes," said Clare, "thank you."

"Then if you will come, I will show you. The room is high

and small, but I think you will be comfortable. Tarquin, you will come in the morning, I expect?"

"Of course."

"Then goodnight."

"Goodnight, Nicola."

They touched cheeks formally, Tarquin went out again and as his sister and Clare went up the stairs, she explained, "This is our family home. I live here while my husband is abroad, with our mother and our two uncles. Zio Lucio is a widower; Zio Paolo never married. Our father is dead; Tarquin is head of the family and he has his own apartments – a villa – near by, and visits Mama every day." She spoke in clear simple Italian, which Clare understood well.

Each closed door on the first floor stood within a deep arch, showing the thickness of the house walls. A more modest stone staircase led spirally up to what appeared to be virtually a separate suit of two rooms and a bathroom opening off a tiny landing. Switching on lights in one of the rooms where there was a made-up bed, Nicola Bernini said, "This was ready for a guest we are expecting. But she does not come for a day or two, so you are welcome to it, *signorina*."

She watched as Clare put down her shoulder bag, and stood, empty-handed, and feeling awkward and forlorn. Then she went on kindly, "You will find towels in the bathroom, and I will lend you some night things of my own – a robe and a nightdress." She paused and looked Clare's figure up and down. "You will find them too ample – we are not at all of the same shape, you and I. And soon they will not be big enough even for me." She paused again, laughed a little self-consciously, and smoothed her generous hips. "You understand, *signorina*? It is no secret. I am pregnant with my first baby. You had not guessed?"

Clare smiled back. "No. When?"

"In the spring. February."

14

"Will your husband be home then?"

"Perhaps. I hope so. He is a pilot – for big oil-ships into narrow harbours. He has to travel and I cannot always go with him. And certainly not while I am *incinta*, as I am now – But I keep you gossiping, and that will not do! I must find you some nightclothes and in the morning Anna, our housekeeper, shall dry and press your own."

She was back again almost as soon as Clare had investigated the bathroom. She brought with her a fine lawn nightgown and a full-sleeved robe which Clare was glad to put on, after taking off her wet dress and slip. The other girl took charge of them, promising, "These you shall have back in the morning. And for the rest, you have what you want – a comb for your hair? Powder? Face cream?"

"In my bag – just a comb and lipstick," Clare told her, hesitating, at a loss to express her gratitude. "You think of everything, *signora*. Why are you so good to me?"

Nicola Bernini smoothed the garments which hung over her arm. "Because I think you are in more trouble than you have told us," she said. "When you joined us, you seemed both angry and frightened, and I think you were glad that you hadn't to go to a hotel for the night. Because you could not pay for it? I ask myself. But of course I do not know."

Clare bit her lip. "I could have paid for a cheap one. It wasn't that – "

"But you would rather not say more?"

For a moment or two Clare was tempted. But again she doubted her ability to make the sordid, complicated story sound credible in her very moderate Italian. For another thing, she felt she hadn't the right to involve these strangers in a dilemma which she must inevitably solve for herself. And for yet another, though she might melt to this girl's kindness and hope for her sympathy, some quirk of pride was revolted by the thought of the story's being passed to Tarquin Roscuro for his judgement on it – and consequently on her own part in it.

So she nodded agreement with the question. "I think I won't," she said. "It's nothing that I can't solve when I go back to Rimini. It's true, I was temporarily stranded when your brother picked me up, but – " She broke off. It all sounded so lame and ungracious, but to her relief her companion seemed to accept it. She said quickly, "Yes, yes. I understand, and I should not wish to press you." She paused as if to give Clare another chance to speak. But when Clare said nothing, she bade her goodnight and left.

Clare took a hot bath, hoping it might help her to sleep, and after a long time, blessedly it did, though her dreams were of leaden-footed attempts to escape from danger; of panic-stricken running and arriving nowhere she recognised; of a man's dark looks and of the sceptical lift of his brows; she was trying to explain something, but the words came out as nonsense . . .

She woke finally to the sound of a knock at her door. An elderly woman, a study in browns, from the dark brown of her cropped hair and the bronze of her deeply-lined face to the nutbrown of overall and apron, came in. She bade Clare a brisk *buon giorno*, set a coffee-tray on the bedside table, laid Clare's newly-pressed things on a chair, opened the window-shutters on to a view of pale blue sky, and withdrew. The Anna of whom Nicola Bernini had spoken, Clare supposed as, full of nervous foreboding, she prepared to face her day.

Nicola Bernini met her on the first-floor landing on her way downstairs, and took her to a small sunny room where a simple breakfast was laid for two.

"Mama and the uncles take breakfast in their rooms, and Tarquin usually goes to see Mama when he comes in. Today he may wish to drive you to Rimini first," Nicola told Clare as she poured coffee and proffered hot rolls and honey, and

16

made friendly, impersonal conversation as if Clare were a conventionally invited guest and she a well-mannered hostess.

They had finished eating but were still at the table when her brother came in. He stooped to kiss her, acknowledging Clare with a bow of his head, but addressing her through Nicola as he began, "I propose to drive Signora Yorke to Rimini before I see Mama – "

"I am 'Miss Yorke' in English. I am not married," Clare put in.

"Ah. I beg your pardon, though we use the title Signora in general," he said. "Meanwhile, if you are ready to go, perhaps you will wait in the car for me?"

Clare thanked Nicola warmly, and they both accompanied her to the door, Tarquin returning to the house when he had seen her into the passenger seat. When he rejoined her he treated her as conventionally as his sister had done at breakfast, asking how she had slept, whether she had been up to San Marino before, and pointing out landmarks as they dropped down to the plain. But when in the city and he had asked her for her destination, his manner changed.

She had prepared her answer. "Please drop me anywhere on the seafront," she said.

"I asked you for your *destination*," he pointed out.

"The seafront will do."

"Abandoning you to the kind of vagrancy from which we rescued you last night?" He shook his head. "Not good enough. When I leave you I intend to do so at some definite address."

"I was *not* a vagrant last night," she denied.

His brief glance at her had the effect of re-clothing her in her drowned rat appearance of overnight. "If you were not, the distinction was a fine one," he remarked cuttingly.

"I was only lost and wet and – !"

" – And, as you've admitted to my sister, in some kind of

17

trouble in a foreign country," he prompted.

She might have known they would have discussed her while she waited in the car! When she said nothing, he went on, "And so, doing any citizen's duty by you, I mean to see you somewhere I consider safe before I leave you. Meanwhile – " he was edging the car into the kerb in front of a restaurant – "we'll stop here for a *cappuccino* while you make up your mind to give me an address, however little more about this trouble you wish to tell me."

Clare did not move. "I do not need coffee. Signora Bernini gave me breakfast," she said.

"Then you can watch me having a cup – which would be unfriendly of you. Please come – "

No longer a drowned rat, but feeling a trapped one, she obeyed. He chose a table under the pavement-awning, ordered two *cappuccinos* and appeared so indifferent to her silence that at last she decided she must break it if they were not to sit there all morning.

"I'm quite all right really, *signore*," she told him. "I'm not destitute, as you seem to think. I have money with me – "

He nodded. "So you told Nicola – money and evening things. But your other possessions, your passport, for instance – where are they?"

She realised he meant to know. "At – at a block of flats in the suburbs."

"Which suburb?"

She told him the district, the name of the street and the rest – "Palazzo Verde, Apartment Sixteen."

"You are living there? It is your home?"

"No. I've been staying there, for about three months. With my – my fiancé's family."

"H'm, rather a far cry from the Via Spezia to where we came upon last night, and from where you seemed unwilling to return to the Palazzo Verde. Instead, without luggage or

18

passport to your name, you wanted a cheap hotel. Why?"

"Because – " She stopped, then tried again. "Because, after what they had done to me, I felt I couldn't trust myself with them – with *any* of them last night. I knew I must face them some time. I – I even want to. But last night I was too angry ... too hurt. I – I *dared* not." She stopped again, appalled at having told this man so much of the humiliation she had meant to keep to herself. Since they had left San Marino they had been speaking in English, and she had the excuse that confidences which she couldn't have expressed in Italian came more easily in her own language. But in her heart she knew his will was using upon her a compulsion which she could not resist.

He was echoing thoughtfully, "After what they had done to you? 'They'? Not 'he'? Your fiancé, I mean?"

"Bruno?" She shook her head. "No, not Bruno alone. They were all in it, and perhaps he may have been involved the least, I don't know – " She heard her voice trail away lamely, and there was a moment's silence before the next inexorable question came.

"And what was it that they did which caused you to leave them so rashly?"

She made an empty gesture. "They – forced me out. But it's all too complicated, and I may have been partly to blame. For – well, hoping too much, for being too eager to be duped. I can't expect you to understand or to sympathise, so please, *signore*, now I've told you the address you wanted, let me go."

He ignored this beating at the bars of her cage. "And when you have bearded this menacing 'them' and have recovered your belongings, what after that for you?"

"I haven't thought yet, beyond what I wanted last night – a cheap room while I collect myself and decide on my next move."

"Disillusioned with some aspect of Italy, you'll be going

19

back to England? You have people of your own?"

"No, no one. Just acquaintances and a few friends. Nor a job. No, I'd hope to get one here and be able to stay for a time."

"Meanwhile, until you get one – if you do – you hang about in Rimini or elsewhere alone. How old are you, *signorina*?"

The abrupt question surprised her. "Twenty. I'm of age in England," she said.

"I know. But the fact isn't exactly a readymade armour for a pretty girl without background."

Embarrassed, she ran a hand under her shoulder-length hair. "I'm not pretty."

His scrutiny was analytical, feature by feature. "You are blonde and blue-eyed and fair-skinned – all acknowledged attractions for the Italian man on the prowl. And at twenty, not only without background, but pretty clearly, without much experience. He finds that a bonus too."

"You don't have to warn me. I can take care of myself!"

"Which you haven't done conspicuously to date – your present plight partly your fault, you say, partly 'theirs'. So much you have admitted under pressure, but it's too little. So what about your now telling me the rest willingly, and allowing me to judge it for myself?"

He was giving her the choice now, not hectoring her, and she gave in. "Well," she began, "it was like this – " and told him.

As he listened he put in a question or two. And when she finished with her headlong flight from Florio Marciano, his expression remained impassive, detached.

To him I'm not "me" at all. I'm a problem that's been thrust on him, thought Clare as, without a word of sympathy, he recapitulated, "So – you were in your third year of hospital training when an injury to your back necessitated an operation, after which your surgeons forbade you to resume nursing for at least two years. You were lonely and depressed at the end of your convalescence in the hospital's seaside home when you met this young musician, Bruno Cavour, on holiday in England. You fell in love."

"I thought I did."

"At twenty it's probably the same thing. And so you let him persuade you to come out to Italy to live with his family – his mother, father and engaged sister – until such time as you married him. You found the prospect exotic and glamorous, and in your innocence an address at a palazzo was akin to a Palladian villa."

Clare bit her lip. "How was I to know that they call high-rise blocks of even small apartments 'palaces' over here?"

"You wouldn't, and if you were as starry-eyed as you say, the fact probably wouldn't have made any difference. No, it was the water-dripping-on-a-stone of your fiancé's family involvement which got you down in the end – his mother's dominance, his father's nonentity and his sister's barely hidden hostility. Do I read the sequence aright?"

"Yes, except that we were never officially engaged. I had no ring. And I'm pretty sure they wore him down first and he was disillusioned about me before I was about him."

"And so, in order to be rid of you, they hatched this plot of compromising you with the man Florio Marciano. He admitted it?"

"Yes. I've told you – he said that once I had spent the night with him, no respectable man would marry me. And of course both Giulia Cavour and Bruno's mother would swear that I had gone out with Florio willingly. That – that was when I hit him," Clare concluded, adding, "But I don't think Bruno was in the plot. I don't *want* to believe so, that is."

"Does it matter, so long as he shares an end-result which he wanted?"

"No, but – " she looked down at her fingers, clasped in her

lap. "I mean, I don't want to think so ill of him, for I did believe I loved him – once. He may have been weak to let his family part us, but they were too strong for him. I see that now, though in England when people warned me, I said 'Fine. I've never had a family of my own, and Bruno's will be readymade.' I never realised the united front that any family can put up against an unwanted outsider. I can still hardly credit that Bruno's family could have done this to me. But I'm forewarned now. Now I know."

"Saying that, finding yourself cheated by one Italian family, next time you are in danger of feeling deeply for someone, you are going to ensure first that he is footloose and wholly family-free?"

As that had indeed been her first angry resolve last night, she went along with it, in spite of the irony in his tone.

"That's right," she agreed a shade too airily. "I shall be more wary lest I leap, as we say in English, out of the frying-pan into the fire. Which means – "

"Thank you, I know what it means," he said coldly. "As we should say in Italian, 'Da il fuomo, ma all' fiamma.' "

She translated slowly, "Out of the smoke, but into the flame. That has the same meaning for you?"

"Exactly. Rather less domestic, but fully as colourful, wouldn't you say?"

"I suppose so, yes."

"Though I'd imagine that only a twenty-year-old could dream of disposing of her own future with any axiom quite so opinionated and glib," he said, and stood, pushing in his chair. "Shall we go now on your errand?" he invited.

She went with him, realising she had been badly snubbed for a generalisation which she should have kept to herself. Not that it had to matter too much what he thought of her, once he had set her down on the Via Spezia ten minutes or so hence ...

But when he parked the car outside the Palazzo Verde and she began to thank him, it appeared he had plans of his own. "Not yet," he said, "I'm coming with you."

That was too much. If he had been less clinical, shown her more sympathy, she might have been glad of his support. But in the ordeal before her she could not bear to have him as a witness of what must be a sordid scene of hostility and recrimination on both sides. As he joined her on the pavement she looked up at him. "No," she said.

"Nonsense. You are not going in there alone."

"I am. It's my problem and I'm handling it myself."

"Who will be there?"

"Probably not Florio Marciano at this hour. But – the rest."

"This Bruno Cavour too?"

"Yes. He doesn't work until the evening."

"It could turn into a brawl."

She shook her head. "It won't. I shouldn't let it. I should come away. But please" – in her urgency she laid a hand on his arm, "– it has got to be just between them and me, without anyone else, any – stranger listening and perhaps taking sides. *Please* don't come with me. Let me go alone!"

He looked down at the hand, then intently into her face. As she looked away at last, embarrassed, he said, "Very well, if you must. I shall wait for you." He got back into the car.

CHAPTER TWO

WHEN, some twenty minutes later, she came out of the building, carrying her suitcase, both he and the car were gone. She drew a sharp breath, staring at the empty kerbside where the car had stood, and experiencing an utterly irrational sense of loss and abandonment which was dangerously near panic.

He had said he would wait, and he hadn't! He had deserted her – because of her obduracy? because she had dubbed him a stranger? even perhaps because he hadn't believed her story, and discretion had told him to leave her to her fate? She thought back over their exchange, at any point of which she would have said she was independent of any help but of the physical escort of his car. She had resented his frosty, non-committal attitude, his disdain of her youthful naïveté; she had thought she could part from him with warm thanks but no regrets.

So why, *why* had she now this sense of deprivation and loneliness; of going begging for the reassurance of one man's notice and company; of wanting, more than anything at this moment, to know that he had kept his promise to be there for her, that he hadn't let her down?

But it seemed he had, and as soon as she had conquered this hollow dropping away of her spirit, she must be on her way alone and as bereft as if Tarquin Roscuro and his kind young sister had never played good Samaritan to her at all.

There was a bus stop at the nearest corner and she had begun to walk towards it when a car swished in to the kerb behind her and, looking back to recognise it, she uttered a long "Oh – " in sheer relief, of which something must have shown in her face. For as Tarquin leaned to open the car door for her, he remarked, "You look as if the lifeboat had arrived in answer to your last rocket. Why? I told you I should be here for you, didn't I?"

"Yes, but I thought – "

"I didn't know what time you might need, and I went to telephone Nicola while I waited. Now I propose to take you back there – to the Casa Torre."

"*Back?*"

"Yes. Nicola has ideas on your subject and wants to see you again." He paused. "How was it?"

She knew he meant her late ordeal. "Rather – horrible," she said.

"You should have let me accompany you."

"No. It was something I had to face by myself."

"And it was as you expected – they were glad to be rid of you?"

"Yes, even Bruno was. That hurt. But the others made it very clear I had never been welcome at all. So I asked permission to pack my things; Giulia Cavour didn't help me, and Bruno didn't offer to see me out, and I can only guess at how gratified they must have been over how well their ploy had worked."

"The thing has embittered you, and you are too young for that," her companion commented.

"Are you suggesting that it would have been easy to take at *any* age?" she retorted.

"No, but the earlier that kind of jaundice sets in, the more cankerous it can be. And the uglier to other people."

"*What* kind of jaundice?"

"Tending to brood on the satisfaction your successful jilting must have afforded these people. Declaring war, as you've done, on the ties of 'family', just because one close-knit family unit declared war on *you* – and won. I admit its methods were bizarre in the extreme, but you are neither the first nor the last twenty-year-old to be betrayed by a love-affair, and if you are wise, you'll put it behind you and forget what you had to pay for the experience."

She was silent under the rebuke of that, hurt that he should think she deserved it, and asking herself why, when she had thought he had disowned her, she should have seen him as her one bulwark against a cruel world. From first to last he had treated her to no spoken sympathy; only with a kind of judicial measurement of all she said and did – and looked, (remembering his deep study of her face after his classification of 'pretty'). He acted for her, but *felt* nothing for her, she suspected. And yet she still wanted to lean on his strength, to have it behind her.

After a while she suggested that perhaps she ought to arrange for some accommodation in the city before he took her back to San Marino. But to that he said, "You may not need to come down again today. You had better see what Nicola wants of you first."

"She didn't say why she wanted to see me again?"

"We discussed it, yes. But she needs to consult you."

Later he asked what kind of a job she had in mind if she stayed in Italy, and she was ashamed at how vague her plans sounded, voiced aloud.

"For a time you could find your lack of fluency in the language a handicap," he suggested.

She agreed, "I know, though I thought perhaps a shop or a tourist agency might take me on. But I realise how fortunate I've been, that you speak and understand English so well. How did you learn it?"

"As you must – if you stay here. By living in the country and having to speak it. My sister may not have told you – our family have been pottery and ceramic makers for generations, and while San Marino didn't enjoy the tourism it has now, we had to seek our markets abroad. I was second in command to my father when he died, but I'd begun at the bottom of the craft, and my experience had to include selling our wares in other countries. I am now the only Roscuro actively in the firm, until any son or sons I may have inherit."

"Signora Bernini mentioned that you have uncles living at the Casa," Clare remarked.

"Yes. But they are both Marinis, our mother's elder brothers. Zio Paolo amuses himself compiling a history of the family, and Zio Lucio's hobby is ballistics – the ancient ones which are some of San Marino's specialities. They are both eccentrics in their way."

By now they had begun the serpentine climb up to the heights above the plain. By night San Marino was sheer fairyland; by day its farms and tiny villages had the neat collected air of a child's table-model, a kingdom in miniature, fashioned for somebody's fun.

Just before they went through the archway to the square, Tarquin pointed out his bachelor quarters, a narrow white house facing out over the valley. Its doorway stood high above the street, up right-and-left flights of stone steps. Its width appeared the narrower by contrast with the long frontages of its neighbours on each side.

"Inside it has more space than you'd think," he explained. "It is a kind of dower-house for the Casa – widowed Roscuro mothers moving over to it when the eldest son marries. Meanwhile I keep it aired for Mama, while she amuses herself planning how she means to make over its decoration when she moves in."

At the Casa Nicola Bernini was waiting for them in a long,

27

elegant room off the fine hall. Her first question puzzled Clare. "Tarquin will have told you?" she asked.

"Told me?" Clare looked from her to her brother, who said, "I've said nothing. I left it to you."

"Oh? Why? It was your plan – " Nicola turned to Clare. "He should have prepared you. You could have been thinking it over. But this is how it is. You will remember that I told you the room where you slept last night was ready for a guest?"

"Yes."

"Well, she is coming by air from England tomorrow. She is sixteen, her name Eirene Landor. She is second cousin to Tarquin and me, great-niece to Mama, but English on her father's side. Mama is aunt to her mother. But now, sadly, there is trouble between these two – Eirene's mother and father – and they have agreed to separate for a time. But they cannot agree as to which of them should have Eirene while they are parted – they suggest, until the spring. And so Tarquin suggested she should come to us, and Mama agreed."

"A slight parallel with the judgement of Solomon," Tarquin put in drily in English. "We airlift the bone of contention to San Marino while the Landors sort themselves out. Which is where you may help," he added to Clare.

"I? How?".

Nicola took up the explanation. "Because Tarquin thought that with my baby coming, I may not be able to take Eirene about later on, so that we need a companion for her. An English girl like herself, young but responsible, and we wonder whether you might join us to help in that way while the child is here?"

For a moment Clare was silent, nonplussed by this offer of an opening which she had no right to expect, and by their readiness, on a few hours' acquaintanceship, to trust her so. She had to be prompted by a crisp "well?" from Tarquin

28

before she collected herself.

Then she told Nicola, "I'm very grateful indeed, and I want to say Yes. But I feel I shouldn't. You've known me for so short a time, and so little about me."

Nicola said with quiet dignity, "But enough, we think." At which Clare demurred. "No. I can give you references – my doctor, the hospital where I worked."

"Don't worry. We'll take them up if we think it necessary," Tarquin promised. "Meanwhile, will you consider the job? If so, decide the salary you expect and we will come to terms."

Nicola said quickly, "Of course you will be joining us as one of us, as one of the family – "

– "Though I think you may find she would prefer to regard herself as our employee," put in Tarquin, the remark having undertones of meaning for Clare which she felt he might have intended. He went on, "I'm not suggesting that Miss Yorke should touch her forelock to us and eat in the kitchen with the staff. I only meant that I think she may expect her status to stop short of any family relationship with us. She will want a contract and stated free times – conditions to be kept by both sides." Then he stood and looked at his watch. "I'll go to Mama now. Where shall I find her?" he asked Nicola, his switch of subject effectually barring any comment from Clare on his highhanded assumption that he knew what she would want of the job.

"Mama? She is sitting on the balcony of her room, I think," Nicola said, and stopped him as he turned away. "I have asked Jaquetta to luncheon. Can you be here?"

"Probably. What time?"

She told him.

"I'll try to be," he said.

When he had gone Nicola worried aloud. "What did he mean? Of course all must be in order for you, but he will see to that. When he rang up to suggest the plan, I saw you as a

29

kind of sister to Eirene, not as a governess or an upper servant, and I hoped that was what you would want."

"And I do," Clare assured her. "I don't know how your brother gained any other impression, for we didn't discuss the idea, which I took to be yours, not his."

"Oh no, it was his. On the telephone he told me your story, and said you wanted work; then he put the plan to me, and asked me to get Mama's approval. Mama agreed, and she is glad you are English, as we think Eirene may not understand much Italian. She is coming through to Rimini Airport tomorrow afternoon. I shall stay to welcome her here, but I think you should go down with Tarquin to meet her. And that's something – " Nicola stopped, as if embarrassed.

"Yes?" Nicola waited.

"Well, about money? Until Tarquin arranges matters with you, have you any? Enough? If not – ?"

Her meaning was clear. What a thoughtful person she was, thought Clare, in thanking her for an offer which she need not take up. She had funds enough for some time, she told Nicola, who then went on to the practicalities of saying that Clare and Eirene would be sharing the little suite in the tower, and as she thought she had heard Tarquin leaving Clare's luggage in the hall, Clare might like to go up and settle in.

In the turret Clare noted with wry interest that the other room, twin to the one where she had slept last night, had been opened up for her. It looked as if the Roscuros had anticipated her acceptance of the job, was her first thought, though her second, more dampening, reminded her that if chance had not thrown her in their way, sooner or later some other English girl would have occupied this room. For even if the notion of engaging her had come from Tarquin himself, he wouldn't have manufactured the post just for her, would he?

She pondered the old-fashioned sound of "companion"?

Would an English teenager want to be furnished with one? And what was the function of a companion to her charge? As friend? As watchdog? As the sister whom Nicola envisaged? Clare decided she was going to have to play it by ear.

When she had unpacked she was glad to get out of the dress she had had to wear since last evening, and into a daydress of brown linen with white saddle-stitching. She changed into low-heeled shoes, meaning, if Nicola had no other plans for her, to explore daytime San Marino in the afternoon. Then she went downstairs, her meeting with Signora Roscuro yet to be faced.

In the hall Nicola was greeting their guest – evidently the Jaquetta of whom she had spoken to Tarquin. From over Nicola's shoulder Clare met the surprised glance of the other girl, who said to Nicola in Italian – perhaps thinking that Clare wouldn't understand her – "Can this be Tarquin's drowned little alien you told me of on the telephone? But why is she still here?"

Nicola laughed and turned, making an introductory gesture between the other two. "Jaquetta – Miss Yorke. Miss Yorke – Signorina Fiore, a friend of ours. Yes, Tarquin had a brilliant idea with regard to Miss Yorke – "

Jaquetta Fiore's eyes narrowed. "*Tarquin* had?"

"As I say," Nicola confirmed, "and so Miss Yorke is joining our household for a while. I must tell you all about it. But let's go to Mama in the *salotto* now, for she hasn't received Miss Yorke yet."

"No?" was Jaquetta's comment on that as, going ahead into the long room where Clare had been interviewed by Tarquin and Nicola, she went to kiss the cheeks of the lady enthroned – there was no other word for the dignity of her pose – on an antique high-backed chair by the window.

"Jaquetta, *cara*. Tarquin is joining us for luncheon, he hopes," Signora Roscuro greeted the younger woman, then offered a graceful beringed hand to Clare. "And you are Signorina Yorke? Nicola has told me about you. Welcome to the Casa Torre, *signorina*. You understand us when we speak Italian?"

Clare touched the hand, reflecting that in using the word "receive" Nicola had chosen the right one. Clare would hardly have been surprised had Signora Roscuro used the royal "we" in speaking of herself, so regal and collected was she, so entirely the great lady.

"*Per lo piu* – mostly," Clare told her in Italian, unable to resist a slanted glance at Jaquetta Fiore as she said it. "There are some phrases and idioms I do not understand. But I am learning."

"Good. How long have you been in Italy?"

"A little over three months."

"Then you have done well, and should improve while you are with us, though you will be using English with our young guest if, as I expect, she will have little Italian." Then, with an air of having concluded the audience, the Signora turned to Nicola. "Shall we not wait for Tarquin? He has not come in yet." She fastened a hand on the head of her ebony stick and rose.

Upright, Emilia Roscuro was not tall, but gave the illusion of being so, her greying dark hair high-piled in a coronet, the carriage of her head superb. Here was the matriarch of her family, thought Clare, ruling it less blatantly than Mama Cavour had ruled hers, but no less its acknowledged queen, with Tarquin as her Regent.

Tarquin appeared as they moved into the dining-room, and at the round table he had Jaquetta Fiore on his right, his mother on his left. The two places between Nicola and Clare were occupied by two elderly men, as squat as their sister was stately, both owl-eyed behind thick spectacles, both seemingly much of an age, both nodding preoccupied greetings to

Clare as Tarquin introduced them to her as his uncles Paolo and Lucio.

Around the table the talk was general, though as it was in Italian and about matters of which she knew nothing, it tended to leave Clare out. She found herself watching them all, particularly contrasting Jaquetta with Nicola, the one a typically Latin beauty, the other as "country cousin" as could be imagined. Jaquetta's complexion had the rich brownish flush of a ripe peach; her eyes were a dark amber; her auburn hair was parted to hang in a heavy swathe over one brow and her gesture in swinging it forward or back was provocative in the extreme. She made use of her hands continually as she talked, their grace adding their own emphasis to what she was saying. Her smile was cool and rather thin, stretching her sensuous lips, but rarely broadening into a full laugh, while Clare watched. Whose friend was she – Nicola's or Tarquin's, Clare wondered, as she was suddenly diverted by a question from the uncle nearest to her – Lucio, she believed, though they were so very alike!

Appearing to think she was a visitor just passing through, he asked her if she would be "there" for the contest for the St. Marinus Pallium three days hence – bewildering her sadly, as she had no idea what the St. Marinus Pallium was.

Tarquin came to her rescue, speaking in English. "Tell him yes," he said. "It is the anniversary day of our foundation as a Republic, when the corps of crossbowmen shoot for the Pallium trophy, and we shall all be there. It's a public holiday – one of our many."

After luncheon Clare excused herself and set out on her tour of the town. She bought a guide-book and sat in the mellow sunshine of the Garibaldi Square to read it and get her bearings with the aid of its map.

When she had visited San Marino with Bruno (odd, that already she could think of him with scarcely a pang), they had come up with the summer crowds and had gone down with them. She hadn't realised, until she now explored its little squares, toiled up its ramps and caught glimpses of its private shaded courtyards, what a gem of a citadel the place was. That other summer afternoon it had been a noisy cosmopolitan bazaar. Today, with autumn in the air, it was quiet, except for a bustling little wind from the south. The people in its streets were its own; the views against the backdrop of the sky were superb; the very stone of its walls and ramparts full of history.

When, tired but enchanted, she returned to the Casa Torre, there was an afternoon silence there too. Nobody seemed to be about, and she was about to go up to her room when her attention was caught by a long framed panel on the wall on the far side of the *salotto* door.

It was not a picture, nor a tapesty. It was an illuminated scroll, its surround in rich colouring, its content a genealogical chart, executed in fine black antique script. From the first entry at the top – "Giulio Roscuro" and a date in the eleventh century – to the last at the bottom – "Tarquin Roscuro" and a birth date thirty-two years back, it was the bare history of a family, the Roscuro family through close on nine centuries from that original Giulio to this latest Tarquin, and nothing beyond him as yet.

Clare's forefinger traced back through Tarquin's name to his father's, Giuseppe Roscuro; to his grandfather's, one Matteo, to his great-grandfather's – Simone Roscuro. That covered around a century of time, and there were eight more behind it –

She started and turned at the sound of footsteps on the marble floor of the hall. It was Tarquin. He came over to her, his glance going from her to the chart.

"Uncle Paolo's work," he said. "You are checking on my family tree?"

"Yes. I noticed it as I came in." She looked back at it. "It goes back a very long way, doesn't it?"

"In the nature of things, families do." His tone was dry. "And in being able to trace ours so far, we're not exceptional. Most Sammarinesi can, probably through our pride in living and dying where we were born."

"Though some of you – the Roscuros – have married foreigners, haven't you?" Clare asked. "For instance" – pointing to the name of a wife in the eighteenth century – "wasn't she German?" And to another – "She sounds English."

"For someone who claims to scorn heritage, you *have* been busy!" His dark eyes mocked her. "Yes, it's true, we're not inbred. We have never had inhibitions against going afield for our women. But we bring them back to our territory; we don't migrate to theirs."

Clare studied the chart again. "It only shows the male line, doesn't it? No younger sons or female branches?"

"No. It is only a father-to-eldest-son tree. If you want the full story, Uncle Paolo will be delighted to show it to you. There's no room here except for followers-on after me."

"Supposing you didn't marry, or only had daughters?"

"That would be too bad. But it hasn't happened to any of us yet. Look" – his fingers beckoned her, "you wouldn't have understood this star beside some of the names?"

Their heads were close as she bent to see. "No. What does it mean?"

"That they served as Captains Regent of the State. We are ruled by two, you know."

Clare remembered the guide-book. "Oh yes. They are elected together and serve for six months at a time, don't they?"

"And while they are in office they are the peers of kings and Presidents the world over. Any male Sammarinese who is over twenty-five can qualify and may serve more than once."

35

Clare pointed to the star beside his own name. "You have been one?"

"Yes. With a stone-mason as my partner. You have come in time to see the next inauguration of Regents in October. It's an even more major occasion than Uncle Lucio's pet shooting-match on Thursday."

"I'll look forward to it." As Clare straightened they were so close and he so tall that her lifting head caught his chin, the impact causing her to stagger and blink starting tears from her eyes.

"I – I'm sorry – "

"Steady," he said, his hands still firm on her upper arms as they both looked over to the hall door where Jaquetta Fiore and Nicola were coming in.

Tarquin and Clare stood apart, but not before Clare had seen Jaquetta's eyes narrow at sight of them together. "We've been to see my dressmaker," Jaquetta said. "How have *you* two spent your afternoon?"

They both answered literally. "At the kilns," said Tarquin, and "I've been looking at the town," said Clare.

"And we believe you – or don't we?" Jaquetta quipped to Nicola, and then claimed desperate hurry. "I must go. Believe it or not, I only came to luncheon! Tarquin, you may see me out. Or, *if* you could spare the time from what looks like a history-lesson, if nothing more intimate, perhaps you would care to drive me home?"

"Of course," he said, and went with her.

At the airport the next afternoon Tarquin and Clare had stationed themselves in sight of the door of the Customs hall when the incoming flight from England had been announced. "I don't quite know what we are looking for," Tarquin remarked, "except for a girl who will be alone."

They waited, watching the passengers filter through –

36

family parties, couples, people singly, but no one alone who could be Eirene Landor. When the stream dried up Tarquin went to look into the Customs hall and returned, shaking his head. "They've all come through. She must have missed the plane," he said.

"Yes. Unless – " Clare looked across to where a young man and a younger girl stood talking and laughing, having left the Customs hall together. The young man was lightly bearded and blond, and wore the accepted uniform of his age-group – parti-dyed jeans and a T-shirt, and he carried his luggage humped like a snail's shell on his back.

As did the girl too, bending slightly forward under the weight of her rucksack. She wore her brown hair in a short gamin cut, and was dressed in a grey flannel blouse with rolled-up sleeves, a brief denim skirt, knee-length socks and bulky canvas sandals. They were so much of a pair that the girl couldn't possibly be Eirene. And yet who else could be?

Tarquin had followed Clare's glance, then looked back at her. "She couldn't have travelled from England like that! Nor have allowed herself to be picked up on the way," he protested.

Clare shook her head. "She could. They do," she said. "Perhaps we ought to see?"

"I suppose so." He went ahead and she followed. He addressed the girl's back. "Miss Landor?"

She turned. "That's me," she said. "Who are you?"

"Tarquin Roscuro, your cousin."

"Oh – yes. And you speak English, thank goodness, for I'm pretty dumb in Italian. Who is this?" – indicating Clare.

"A Miss Yorke, who is English herself and whom we've asked to stay while you are with us."

"Thank goodness for that, too." Eirene's surprisingly child-like and dimpled smile approved Clare. Then she went on, "Well, now we're all acquainted – except Frank. Tarquin,

37

Miss Yorke – meet Frank, will you?"

Tarquin looked the young man up and down. "A friend?" he asked icily.

"Well, yes – and no. We just met on the plane. He has come to see if he'd like to work for his uncle in Rimini. He – "

But Frank, clearly uncomfortable under Tarquin's uncompromising stare, scuffed the toe of his sandal on the floor, muttered, "So I'll be on my way. Nice meeting you, Eirene – " sketched a salute between the three of them, and loped away.

Eirene looked her reproach at Tarquin. "You scared him off, and he was nice. Still, we exchanged addresses, so I can get in touch."

"What is his other name?"

She giggled. "D'you know, I didn't ask!"

"Useful, having his address, if you don't know his name," was Tarquin's dry comment.

"So what? I've got his telephone number too, so can't I ring and just ask for Frank?" She jerked upright as Tarquin gestured to the pack on her back. "What do you want?"

"That. Take it off," he ordered.

"But I can't. It's all *balanced*!"

"Take it off. In our country women don't carry burdens of that size while men go emptyhanded."

"Oh, all right." She shrugged herself out of the holding straps and handed the rucksack over. He took the weight of it with three fingers under a loop. "This way to the car park. Come along," he said, ignoring her stage-whisper to Clare, "Isn't he *masterful*? And chivalrous? Does he come all over alike with you too?"

Sitting beside Clare in the back of the car, she seemed to approve what she saw of Rimini as they drove through it. But when they left it behind and began the long climb to San Marino, she affected an accent to ask, "Wot? No beach? Where do we swim?"

38

"Not from any beach in San Marino," Tarquin told her. "You would have to go down to Rimini."

"How far will that be? And how does one *get*?"

"Twelve kilometres. That's about eight English miles. You could be brought down by car, or there's a bus service every day. But won't the swimming season soon be over?"

"M'm, I suppose so. So what else can one find to do on the top of your sugar-loaf of a mountain?"

"That," said Tarquin evenly, "you must decide for yourselves. Miss Yorke has only been with us two days herself, so you can go on voyages of discovery together."

Eirene turned to Clare. "Is that so? You're just out from England too?"

Clare shook her head. "No, I've been in Rimini for three months. But I was out of a job, and I came up to San Marino when Signor Roscuro offered me this one as an English companion for you."

Eirene wrinkled her nose. "A companion? How stuffy! Why can't we just be friends?"

"I hope we're going to be," said Clare, warming to her for all her brashness, though wondering a little how it might be received in the somewhat rarefied atmosphere surrounding their queenly hostess. Clare doubted whether Signora Roscuro's vision of her great-niece would quite measure up to the reality which Eirene was.

When they arrived, they stood outside the car while Tarquin was taking Eirene's pack from the boot. Eirene looked with distaste at the house; at its stern granite walls, its shaddowed portico, its small shuttered windows, and craned her neck to peer at the turret which gave it its name.

"Gosh! I've seen prisons that were positively festive by contrast," was her comment. "And to think that I might have to spend the whole winter here, while –" She broke off, frowning. "How am I going to bear it? How can *you*?"

39

But Clare, looking at the same grey walls, saw only the golden light which the early evening sun was casting across them, and remembered the kindness there had been for her behind them. "I can, I think," she said. "And you could find that the whole place grows on you after a while. It's doing it already to me. It's rather like an eagle's eyrie – safe."

"*Safe!*" scorned Eirene. "Who wants to be safe?"

I believe I do, thought Clare, surprising herself. But she did not say so aloud.

CHAPTER THREE

FOLLOWING Eirene's appearance in the Roscuro family circle, Clare felt its members deserved full marks for the acceptance of their trendy young relative.

Tarquin's initial reaction of shock had been the least well concealed. Nicola, after one bewildered blink of recoil, offered both hands in the warmest of welcomes and suffered a bear-hug with admirable calm. Signora Roscuro, who used spectacles on a neck-chain with the elegant handling she would have accorded a lorgnette, raised them to her eyes, lowered them, and offered her cheek without a tremor to the onslaught of her great-niece's smacking kiss.

The uncles, meeting Eirene for the first time at dinner that night, appeared to take her arrival in their preoccupied stride as they had taken Clare's. Two new young people added to the household at a stroke? It was all one to them, their manner seemed to say, though Paolo, grasping Eirene's relationship to him, gave her a recital of her mother's antecedents three generations back, before retiring again into his shell. Lucio barely emerged from his.

Meanwhile Eirene, mixing broken Italian and vigorous English, was establishing herself as a force to be reckoned with.

Yes, she had left school. School was a drag. No, she couldn't translate "drag"; they must take it from her that it *was*.

She wished it were summer instead of winter ahead. How cold was cold in Italy? And what did people do when it was? Yes, she loved Italian food. There were Italian restaurants in London. All those lovely squiggly *pastas*! And Italian ice-cream – yummy!

Her final edict before the party adjourned to the *salotto* for coffee and talk and some television was to the effect that she had no intention of calling Clare "Miss Yorke". Nor need Nicola, nor Tarquin, surely? Any more than Tarquin and Nicola had to be "Signor Roscuro" and "Signora Bernini" to Clare? First names were so much more matey. Well, weren't they? she appealed. And Clare was one of the family – well, sort of, wasn't she?

Tarquin sent a glance at Clare. "You'd better consult Miss Yorke as to that," he said, speaking directly to her, not to Eirene.

"*Clare*!" Eirene insisted.

"Not until she has said we may. Well, Miss Yorke?"

"Of course," Clare agreed, flushing against her will, as Signora Roscuro offered her considered opinion that it sounded an excellent idea to her, so long as nobody but her own contemporaries expected to call her "Emilia" to her face – which was a touch of tolerant humour as unexpected as it was welcome to Clare. The great lady was human, after all!

Eirene had approved of the turret suite as "quite cosy, considering" – warmer praise than she had given the outside of the house. When they retired to it at the end of the evening, she left her door open in order to talk to Clare, and came across in her dressing-gown to sit on Clare's bed and to demand, "And so what happens next – tomorrow, I mean, and the tomorrows after that?"

"Well, I expect you'd like to explore the place," said Clare. "I did a bit yesterday, and it's unique in its way."

"Are there any shops? Decent ones?"

42

"Quite a lot of choice, though I noticed some had closed for the winter. I found the streets and the houses rather fascinating, and there are museums and art galleries, and the Basilica is really beautiful."

"Uh-huh? 'Fraid I don't go much for culture," confessed Eirene. "Any discos in sight? And what's this Pallium thing they were talking about after dinner?"

"It's a kind of shooting match. It happens on Thursday."

Eirene's interest was sparked. "A clay pigeon shoot? I've been to some, and they're rather fun. Or shooting at those balls bubbling up on water, like at a fair?"

"Neither, I think," said Clare. "As far as I can gather it's a ceremony in costume that they are bound to hold on their Foundation Day, and the shooting is at targets with 'way back ancient weapons like crossbows. There are nine castles round about on the hills, and they all compete for this Pallium, which I suppose could be a flag."

"And they make a day of it, do they? Whoopee, and all that? I could ask Frank to get his uncle to bring him up for it, couldn't I?" mused Eirene. "What do you think they would say if I did?"

" 'They' being your people?" Clare questioned. "You'd have to ask your great-aunt or – Tarquin." The name came unreadily to her lips.

"*You* ask Tarquin for me," Eirene coaxed. "He seemed to think Frank had the darkest of designs upon me, but if you tell him we'll be chaperoned by you and this uncle, he could agree. After all, he must have seen you as a worthy type, or he wouldn't have booked you to look after me. Though am I glad he did! What kind of job were you doing before you took me on?"

"I didn't have one in Italy."

"But I thought you said – ?"

"That I'd been out here some time? But that was with the

43

prospect of getting married, not to a job."

"Getting *married*?" Eirene settled herself more comfortably, cross-legged and holding the toes of her slippers. "Tell – !"

Clare told her, to the accompaniment of her shocked exclamations and sympathetic coos. "Well, there's a thing!" she commented finally. "And Tarquin coming to the scene in the nick of time, riding in like a knight over the horizon – "

"Not Tarquin only. Nicola came to my rescue too," Clare amended.

"But it was Tarquin who cooked up the job for you – "

"He did *not* 'cook it up'! They needed someone English for you, and I – well, I just happened along."

"Bet he wouldn't have taken you on if, say, you'd been a hippy type or had a voice like a corncrake." Eirene tilted her head and studied Clare. "D'you think maybe he *fancies* you?" she asked.

"Fancies me? Of course not! He's only known me for round about seventy-two hours."

"Well, do you fancy *him*?"

"For the same reason – that I've only known him for as long as he's known me – no," said Clare, adding a shade too sharply, "You're talking nonsense, do you know that? Go to bed."

Slowly Eirene unfolded her convolutions and slid to the floor. "You don't have to go spare just because I asked an innocent question," she grumbled. She went out, closing the door behind her, but a second or two later she was back, putting her head round it. "Forgiven? Pax?" she asked anxiously.

Clare smile. "Forgiven. Pax," she echoed. "Goodnight."

Later, before she slept, it occurred to her that though she had told Eirene about her circumstances, the girl had offered no confidences of her own in return, and Clare wondered how much impact the differences and trial separation of a mother and father might have on a daughter of sixteen. Would she

44

take sides? Or would she find herself torn between them? Or, if the sadness of it affected her not at all, how insensitive must she be?

Clare herself had no way of knowing. Two years before she was sixteen she had lost her father, and her mother had died two years before that. From her teens until she began her nursing training she had lived with a widowed aunt, who had since remarried and gone to America. So Clare had only a child's memory of a loving relationship which, so far as she knew, had never had the seeds of discord in it, which didn't help her to gauge how much or how little Eirene might have suffered from her parents' break-up. Certainly she was cheerful and extrovert and she hadn't shown any signs of playing for sympathy. Except – Clare had suddenly remembered how, at her first dismayed sight of the Casa, Eirene had frowned and clenched her jaws, as a child might, fighting a lump in the throat which threatened to betray her to tears. But she had caught herself back from contemplating the likely length of her exile in San Marino, and hadn't mentioned or appeared depressed by its prospect since.

Sleepy now, Clare wondered if she were making for herself a problem which didn't exist for Eirene's teenage capacity for resilience. And from that did it follow that caring deeply and perhaps suffering unbearably in consequence increased as you grew up further, became more adult, more aware? Were the smug people who counselled the young, "You'll soon get over it," always right? Just because they were older, *did* they know it all?

True, Tarquin Roscuro had said as much to her, and he had been right – about the shrivelling of whatever love she had had for Bruno Cavour. But about the scars which the experience had inflicted on her – ?

She was asleep without having worked out the answer to that one.

Much later still she woke again, roused by some sound which she couldn't at first define. She sat up in bed and listened. The sound continued, regular as a snore as someone drew sleeping breath. But it wasn't snoring. It was sobbing, and from quite near by – from Eirene's room across the little landing. Clare was up and across her room, softly opening her door and listening at the other one.

Eirene was crying. But was it only in her sleep, or was she awake? Clare bit her lip and thought. If the girl were asleep, she wouldn't know she was doing it. And she *sounded* asleep, so regular were the sobs. If she were awake – But on the impulse to go in and comfort her, Clare paused.

Supposing it were she at sixteen, who hadn't confided her desolation to anyone, would she want anyone to guess? Clare knew that, whether or not you suffered hurt for long, at that age, *while* you suffered it there were fronts to be kept up, prides to maintain. At sixteen, if you blubbed and did it on somebody's shoulder, later you were ashamed and couldn't face them. Which went too for any weeping you did later, when experience should have taught you the poise which wouldn't allow it.

And so Clare didn't open Eirene's door and go in. She waited, still indecisive and shivering nervously, until the sobbing stopped and there was silence. She waited a little longer still, then went back to bed, feeling that wisely or unwisely she had "saved face" for Eirene. And saving face, when you were young, was important ...

The next morning, Eirene, today in a rainbow-coloured smock, bare-legged and draped with waist-length beads, was so much herself again that Clare was glad she had not gone to her in the night. After breakfast Clare suggested they might help in the house, but Nicola said this was not necessary, and Eirene demanded to be shown the town and the shops.

In the town, which was being hung with flags for the next

46

day's holiday, Eirene, arguing that it was a free country and that Tarquin couldn't actually *eat* Frank if she invited him to the Pallium, asked Clare to help her to telephone him. Clare got the number for her in a public kiosk and left her to it. It appeared, when she had talked to him, that Frank's surname was Bridgeman, as was his uncle Oscar's too; that they accepted the invitation and would call at the Casa Torre when they arrived – crash tactics which Clare rather deplored, but which she could hardly veto on her own authority.

"I'll be all right," Eirene argued comfortably. "The greybeard uncle will make it respectable, and Frank has to have him along as transport, though Frank means to get a scooter and be independent. I could hire a scooter too, and we could go about together, couldn't we?"

"Though I doubt whether a scooter for you on these heights would be very popular with your people," Clare demurred. "Anyway I thought Frank had come to work for his uncle? What does the uncle do?"

But Eirene didn't know that, though she believed he was "buying land or something". She next turned her attention to the shops, looking and lingering and pricing – mostly at the souvenir and imitation jewellery displays on each shop's apron of pavement.

She was trying on "silver filigree" rings and bracelets to match at one of these latter, and Clare was warning that they might look very tawdry when she got them home, when a shadow fell across the stall, and Clare looked up to face Jaquetta Fiore.

"I thought it was you, Miss Yorke," she said. Though she had spoken Italian entirely at the Casa, she now used English – carefully and with a marked accent which Clare had to allow was rather attractive. "And this will be the young Eirene from England, to whom, Nicola tells me, you are to be – " she hesitated, then had recourse to Italian – "*gouvernante*?"

47

None too flattered by the term, Clare began, "Well, not exactly 'governess' – " But Jaquetta had already turned her cool smile upon Eirene and was offering her hand. "I have heard about you from Tarquin," she told the girl. "My name is Jaquetta Fiore. You may often see me at the Casa Torre. Tarquin – and Nicola – are great friends of mine." Then her glance fell on the hand she held in hers and she gasped. Eirene's fingers were still adorned with three or four flashy rings and her wrist with two bangles.

"*Cara mia*, you cannot think of buying this – " again she needed to use "*robaccia*" for "rubbish". But Eirene evidently understood her tone. Withdrawing her hand from Jaquetta's, she spread her fingers and turned the bracelets with her other hand.

"What's wrong with it?" she defended. "It's gay and bright and *marvellously* cheap!"

"But – !" Jaquetta turned to Clare, thin-lipped, her smile gone. "She has not bought it yet? You have not allowed it? You should know better, surely?"

Stung, Clare managed to say quietly. "No, she was only looking at it."

"Then make her take it off! Yes, off! Off!" Jaquetta demanded, the flutter of her expressive hands emphasising every word. And when Eirene, shamefaced, had slowly obeyed, Jaquetta tucked her arm in hers and urged, "Now we shall go and look at something much better. For we make some beautiful jewellery in San Marino, and I shall buy you a piece. So come along. Yes, you too, Miss Yorke," she added over her shoulder to Clare as she went ahead with Eirene. Rather as if I ought to sit up and beg to be allowed to go with them! thought Clare savagely as she followed.

Jaquetta's objective was a jeweller's shop in a side street, its sole wares on display in the tiny window being one diamond necklace carelessly a-sprawl on black velvet. But within, the place was an Aladdin's cave of brilliance. Clare heard Eirene murmur a half-whispered, "Oh no!" But Jaquetta had seated herself in the chair brought forward for her and was asking to be shown gold bracelets. "A gift for the *signorina*," she said in an aside to the assistant, which Clare took to mean that the prices were not to be mentioned in front of Eirene.

Obviously bedazzled, Eirene tried several on her wrist, but went back more than once to the very slim ones which the salesmen said were meant to be worn two or three together. "The young *signorinas* like the music they make – jingle, jangle," he pointed out. Upon which Jaquetta decided, "Then we shall take three," told the man to enter them to her account and asked they shouldn't be parcelled, as she was sure Eirene would prefer to wear them.

Clearly Eirene did prefer so, though she made some appropriate noises of "You shouldn't," and "I ought not to," which Jaquetta brushed aside. Outside again, she said, "Now you must come home with me for morning coffee. I live below, outside the walls – " she waved a hand towards the valley – "but it is all downhill and not far."

Ten minutes' walking brought them to some avenues of modern villas, pantiled in blues and greens and pinks and white-walled, in sharp contrast with the uniform weathered grey granite of the older town. Jaquetta's home was one of three, grouped about a central lily-pond, bordered by young cypresses, and in the garden behind it was a small swimming-pool which brought an "Oo-h" of pleasure to Eirene's lips.

"You like to swim?" smiled Jaquetta.

"Very much. But Tarquin said I couldn't. Or rather, that of course there wasn't any sea."

"Then I shall scold him. He should have remembered our pool," said Jaquetta. "At any time when you would like to swim, you have only to ask or to come. We keep it warmed to twenty-five degrees in the winter," she added carelessly over

Eirene's delighted thanks.

Over coffee, which they took on a terrace, they managed polite conversation in mixed Italian and English, Jaquetta usually and rather pointedly addressing Eirene, but occasionally forced to appeal to Clare to interpret for her. Clare had just decided it was time they left when a door from the house opened and Jaquetta's father came out.

Signor Fiore was a big, heavy-jowled man with hard eyes, whose interest in his daughter's guests was minimal, once introductions had been made. He accepted a cup of coffee, but drank it standing while he talked to Jaquetta in rapid Italian, and left when he had put down his cup. "Papa is so occupied with business," Jaquetta murmured, excusing him, as Clare rose and said they must be going.

"I shall drive you back," offered Jaquetta.

But Clare said No. They had come out for the morning, meaning to walk. But they hadn't done much and they would like to walk back. "Oh, very well," Jaquetta shrugged. She offered her hand to Clare, but kissed Eirene on both cheeks. "*Ciao, cara mia*," she said. "I shall see you at the Pallium tomorrow?"

On the way back Eirene was ecstatic about the encounter, and of Jaquetta – wasn't she *lovely*? That hair – its colour and the way it swung – just out of this world! And the way she used her hands – they positively talked. Eirene's few passes with her own hands were neither expressive nor graceful, but they served to set her new bracelets jangling, and she was still flinging them round and round her wrist when they encountered Tarquin at the door of the Casa as he was about to go in.

"You've been shopping," he said, nodding towards the bracelets.

"Yes! That is, no. We met a friend of yours, Signorina Fiore, and she bought them for me – Look!"

Tarquin took the hand she offered to him and bent to look

closely. Then he glanced up at her, and at Clare. "But these are gold," he said, not smiling. "Valuable – "

Eirene drew back her hand, shuffling the trinkets down to her wrist. "I know," she said hesitantly. "But she *would* – "

"Would what?"

"Buy them for me."

"And you accepted them?"

"Well, she insisted. And I did want them. Was that very wrong?" Eirene appealed.

Tarquin compressed his lips. Then – "Plainly not in your eyes. And you've got them, haven't you?" he said.

"And I may keep them? You're not angry? Signorina Fiore – she asked me to call her Jaquetta – was so *nice*. And isn't she quite, quite beautiful? I wish – " Eirene babbled happily on as he opened the door for them and followed them in, signalling with a forefinger to Clare to halt her, when Eirene raced away "to show Nicola," she claimed.

Tarquin said nothing until she was out of hearing. Then he told Clare, "You should have known better than to allow her to take a present of that value from Jaquetta Fiore. You should have declined it for her. *You* have enough Italian to make yourself clear – politely. Eirene has not, and you should have intervened."

Clare felt this to be unjust. "I doubt if Signorina Fiore would have listened if I had," she said. "As Eirene has told you, she was very insistent. She had been shocked at Eirene's choice of imitation jewellery, and I wasn't to know that you would mind if she bought her something better."

"Something better! Gold worth thousands of lire? Even if Jaquetta had offered it, you could have discouraged Eirene from accepting it."

Clare had to bite back her impulse to retort that she was not Eirene's keeper, for she was learning from this exchange that in his eyes, this was just what she was. Instead she parried,

"And risked offending Signorina Fiore, who claimed enough intimacy with you and your sister to let me suppose she had the right to make such a present to Eirene?"

"*A* present, perhaps. But not one of such value."

Clare said stiffly, "Neither Eirene nor I were allowed to learn its value. The salesman didn't mention it, and the things were entered to the Signorina's account."

"I'd have expected you to make a guess."

"I did guess – "

"Yet you didn't question the desirability of accepting such an extravagant gesture?"

"Made to myself, of course, I should have refused it. As it was made to Eirene from a close friend of yours, I didn't think I had the right to interfere." After pausing, she heard the pertness in her tone as she continued, "So what do you want me to do now? Tell Eirene that she can't keep the bracelets, that she must return them?"

The movement of Tarquin's shoulder was impatient. "Of course not. That would be to make more of the affair than it's worth."

"Then if so, haven't you made rather too much of it to me?"

"Perhaps. Though not, I think," he said coolly, "if I've underlined your responsibilities towards Eirene; the kind of balance we expect from you, which clearly she hasn't yet learnt."

"I see. At just four years' difference between us? In other words, for 'companion', read 'duenna' – or whatever the equivalent Italian is?"

He nodded. "In other words, for 'companion' read 'duenna'," he echoed.

"Thank you. As long as I know – "

"Though I think we can settle for 'companion' in English and '*camerata*' in Italian and hope for the same results," he

52

said, his unexpected smile disarming her, inviting her reluctant smile in return. It was not until after much later pondering that she thought she had a clue to why he might have taken so much offence at Jaquetta's too-expensive gift to Eirene. He hadn't rounded so sharply on Clare herself, merely to recall her to her duties towards the girl, she was sure. More likely, she thought, it was his male Latin pride being a little jealous of Jaquetta's quixotic show of liberality towards *his* young relative. Naturally, in the intimacy which Jaquetta claimed with him and which he didn't deny, he wouldn't admit as much to her, Clare decided. And so he had made her the scapegoat for his pique against Jaquetta.

Unfair of him, of course. But it made him oddly vulnerable. If it were so, it showed that, beneath his iron exterior, he could bleed . . .

Although he had no official status in the affair, on the day of the Pallium Lucio Marini came into his own. When he left early for the Cesta Tower, on the ramparts of which the contest was to be held, he invited Clare and Eirene to go with him, and he would show them round the Armoury before the crowds arrived.

Clare accepted, but Eirene declined, reminding Clare that Frank Bridgeman and his uncle were calling for them at some unspecified time of the morning.

"Who wants to see a lot of rusty old guns, anyway?" she demanded.

Clare said, "I doubt if they'll be rusty. I understand your uncle Lucio has carte blanche from the authorities to group and tend and polish them any time he likes. But I probably needn't be more than an hour, and if Frank arrives before then, you'll have to entertain him and his uncle yourself."

"Under the eagle eye of Great-Aunt Emilia, who'll be looking *through* them? She wanted to know whether my parents knew Frank, and she only agreed to 'receive' him, as she calls it, when Nicola told her that Tarquin and you had met him," Eirene grumbled. "At least Tarquin didn't object when he heard he was bringing his uncle Oscar along. But for me, you can't get back too soon to rescue me from having to *explain* them to the family."

As soon as Lucio had launched Clare on her tour of the Armoury, she realised how sadly she had underestimated the time needed to do it justice. For it housed a fascinating collection of armours and weapons of from centuries back to specimens used in the latest of twentieth-century wars.

There were suits of mail, pikes, cuirasses, cannon, pistols, hand-missiles, even pitchforks and digging tools. The guardrooms themselves were preserved as they had been at the time of the Tower's building in the thirteenth century, the second of San Marino's crag-top fortresses, the Guaita, the Cesta and the Montale. Here were the great hooded fireplace where the guardsmen would warm themselves and "brew up" between guard-stands, drinking-horns, pewter platters, bullseye lanterns and copper cooking-pots.

Ably guided by Lucio, Clare moved about, looking and fingering, and peopling in her imagination these rooms with the soldiery who would have used these plates, drunk from these horns and warmed themselves at this grate . . . Roscuros among them, there must have been, and when she said so to Lucio, he confirmed that with enthusiasm.

"There have always been Roscuros in San Marino – always," he declared. "Ask my brother Paolo about them – he knows. Marinis too, but our family was Italian-born. We haven't as deep roots in San Marino as the Roscuros have."

He excused Clare willingly when she told him she must go. He too, he said, must busy himself helping with the weaponry for the afternoon's contest. But she must come again – there was still much he could show and tell her, he said, and added a compliment which pleased her – "The pretty ones like you, *signorina*, are not always so willing to listen to what an old man like me has to tell them, and I am flattered that you should."

There was no car outside the Casa when Clare arrived back there, so she concluded she was in time to effect Eirene's "rescue". Eirene met her in the hall, worrying, "I hope they'll come soon, while Aunt Emilia is still in her room and Tarquin is out. I don't know where Uncle Paolo is, so that only leaves Nicola for them to face. And you will get her to let them take us out, won't you? Oh, hark, that was a car stopping, wasn't it?"

It was – a small open runabout of Italian make, with a noisy engine and few pretensions to grace. When Eirene opened the door Frank vaulted out and the driver followed him. Eirene looked from one to the other. "Two of you?" she puzzled. "But where is your uncle?"

Frank nudged his companion forward. "Here," he said.

"Where? You said – "

The other man, in appearance no more than five or six years older than Frank, laughed. Looking beyond Eirene to Clare, "True," he told them both. "Sorry if you were expecting a senior citizen, but it's just one of those quirks of relationship that happen – by my having arrived late in my father's marriage, by which time young nephew Frank wasn't far behind. No more difference than made me Bridgeman One and him Bridgeman Two at school." He turned to Frank. "Come on, man, do your stuff. Introductions all round."

Frank looked doubtfully at Clare. "I don't – " he began.

"Yes, you *do*," Eirene put in. "At the airport Tarquin told us she was Miss Yorke. But she isn't any longer; she is Clare; and I am Eirene, and you are Frank and Oscar – You don't call him Uncle Oscar, do you? No? Fine. Then come now and meet Nicola, my other second cousin. She is married, but her husband is away. Besides her, there are my great-aunt Emilia and two great-uncles. But you don't have to take them all at one gulp. I don't think they're around just now."

While Eirene was talking Clare was adjusting her ideas of the expected "greybeard uncle". Oscar Bridgeman was a slightly more mature edition of his nephew – blond, easy-limbed with an open smile. As they all went into the house, he remarked to Clare, "So our family is not the only one that's a bit complicated. Eirene sounds as if hers might pose a problem or two, too." Upon which, overhearing, Eirene threw at him over her shoulder, "And you can say that again! What's more, ours goes back for centuries, they tell me, and my uncle Paolo can tell you exactly when every man jack of us was born!"

They met Nicola at the door of the *salotto*. She had the young men's relationship explained to her and she asked them to coffee which, Oscar, as spokesman, declined in quite passable Italian, saying he hoped they might drive the girls on a tour of the town to see the decorations and take them to luncheon before the contest.

After a moment's hesitation Nicola said yes, that would be all right.

"And you will be there yourself, *signora*?" Oscar asked politely.

Nicola said she thought not, this year. Her mother would not be going; they had both seen many Pallium contests, and they would stay at home together. "Have you seen one yourself before, *signore*?" she asked.

Oscar said he had not. He had only been in Italy for a few months.

"You are not on holiday? I think Eirene said you have business interests in Rimini? Is that so?"

He hoped to develop some, but he had none as yet, Oscar said, which accounted for his present leisure, thought Clare, though remembering that Eirene had said vaguely that he was

56

"in land or something" and that Frank had come out to Italy to work for him.

Outside again Frank, who had a tourist's licence, asked if he might drive, and did so, with Eirene beside him. Clare and Oscar shared the none too ample room of the back seat. As the little car bucketed and plunged round the narrow streets Frank frequently lost his way. "The darned place is like a maze. You aren't *meant* to arrive anywhere you want to be," he declared.

"Where is the best place to lunch?" Oscar wanted to know. But of course neither girl could tell him, so he chose one in the high town, just below the Guaita Tower, which gave a whole panoramic view of the plain below. The menu was choice and typically of the rich Romagna region, with overtones of San Marino specialities in the way of wines and desserts.

They had been early, and had been given a good table in one of the window-bays. Those in the other bays had been marked Reserved, and it was to one of these that Tarquin, escorting Jaquetta Fiore, was shown later, when Oscar's party was about halfway through their meal. Eirene saw the other two first and waved to Tarquin, who halted, spoke briefly to Jaquetta and brought her over.

Oscar and Frank stood, and Eirene made the introductions. Tarquin's sharp, questioning look at Oscar did not escape Clare. Clearly his reaction to Oscar's obvious youth matched her own and Eirene's – as if there were a minimum age for uncles, below which they shouldn't exist, she thought amused-ly, as Jaquetta used her charm on both males and teased Eirene lightly that, at the girl's age and Clare's, *she* could not have lunched out at a restaurant with two men. But the English had such different ideas, didn't they? Not that she minded having been so sheltered. It made one's later emergence from the schoolroom so much more exciting, and the men that *little* bit more appreciative – "Ask Tarquin", she had concluded with a provocative glance his way.

But no one did ask Tarquin, and when they had returned to their own table, Frank grumbled, "First time I've heard I shouldn't offer a girl to share a nosebag with me at midday!"; Eirene murmured, "Yes, but isn't she a *looker*?" and Oscar muttered, frowning, "Fiore? Fiore? I'm hoping to do business with a chap of that name. I wonder if he could be Signorina Fiore's father?"

After luncheon they set out for the Cesta ramparts, but owing to the crowds, had to park the car some distance from the Tower and walk up to it. They found good places behind the barricades, and were in time for the military band parade which led the procession of the competing crossbowmen, clad to a man in colourful mediaeval costume and headed by the purple, gold and white San Marino standard.

First of all there was a ceremony of homage to the crossbow-men's patron saint, their oath of loyalty to the State and an address to the assembled guests. Then they went to their emplacements; each team's heavy weapons were loaded and cocked in turn, and a succession of finely-tempered, iron-tipped missiles went flatly-winging to the distant target.

Though the crowds were enthusiastic and loud in their comments on the finer points of the game, to the English party the rules were complicated and the arguments going on around them incomprehensible. It was Eirene who first became restive. "It's a bit like a regatta, when the chap who looks to be behind all the rest turns out to be in the lead, surprise, surprise," she grumbled. "Do you know, I've about *had* this shooting caper? Isn't there anything else we could do?"

Frank was only too ready to agree with her, though Clare and Oscar were intrigued enough to want to see the contest out. Frank asked Oscar, "Well, may I have the car again and take Eirene out into the country for a spin? We could meet up later – say, in an hour? – if you'll name the place?"

Clare, over-conscious now of Tarquin's ideas of her duty to Eirene, began, "Well – " But Oscar, seeming to think she was questioning Frank's driving, said, "Not to worry. On the whole he's a better driver than I am. Let's let them go. And what is that open square in the town centre where we might meet?"

"Near the Government House? Liberty Square," Clare told him.

"Then Liberty Square in an hour, and be late at your peril," Oscar warned Frank, who lifted a thumb in agreement and began to push a way for Eirene through the crowds.

The other two returned their attention to the contest which, from the mounting excitement around them, seemed to be nearing a climax. Clare, worrying aloud, "I wish we understood the scoring better," suddenly spotted Uncle Lucio, a privileged person evidently, within the arena itself. He stood immediately below them, his shoulder within touching distance of a hand put through the barricades. Clare thrust hers through and at her touch he looked up.

"Ah, Signorina Clare!" he smiled. "You enjoy the contest? You know there is only one more round to be shot, and the Pallium is won?"

Clare shook her head. "We don't understand it very well. I was going to ask you – "

"But of course! Wait! I will come to you and explain it all!"

As good as his word, he squeezed in beside them a few minutes later; brought with him a chart showing the markings and penalties, indicated which team was likely to win, which might be the runner-up, and which was the hopeless loser, and stayed with them until the last round had been fired and the winning team proclaimed.

They stayed to see the presentation of the Pallium, which was not a flag, but a richly embroidered cloth which might have been either a stole or a banner. Then, as the crowd began to disperse, they went with it and down to Liberty Square.

They were early for the rendezvous, so they sat on the parapet, talking over the afternoon and exchanging personal details for which there had been no time until then.

Clare told briefly why she had come out to Italy, of her understanding with Bruno Cavour which clearly wasn't going to work, but not of her humiliation which had ended it. Hoping to be able to stay on in Italy, she had been glad to get her present job, she said. The Roscuro family had been kind and had made her welcome, and Eirene – well, from what Oscar had seen of Eirene, wouldn't he agree that she was likely to keep any "companion" on her toes?

Oscar's immediate history was that he had held a junior post in an English estate agency when he had been left a considerable legacy by his maternal grandfather. He had been faced with a choice of either buying himself a partnership in the firm or of indulging his dream of owning and administering a property estate, preferably "somewhere in the sun", and had been tempted to Italy, where the prospects were wide open if the land could be bought at a favourable price. He was in touch with various firms with land for sale; thought he would probably deal with that of Giovanni Fiore, and had suggested that Frank, who had only just scraped through his A-level exams, and didn't want to go to college, should join him for a few months with a view to his assistance when the deal went through and Oscar's residential building began.

It was a gamble, he admitted, but while he was a bachelor he had no commitments nor responsibilities to anyone, and if the scheme got under way at all, it would be worth the risk, and if it failed, both he and Frank must see it as experience bought.

"And you think Jaquetta Fiore may be connected with this Fiore firm?" Clare queried. "I've met her father – a big, heavy man, not very outgoing."

"That's the chap, for sure. I imagine he'll drive a very hard bargain, but he seems to command the best land on the market. What is it with his daughter and Eirene's cousin Tarquin? Are they engaged?" asked Oscar.

"I don't know. No one has said so. Why do you ask?"

"No reason really, except that she struck me as being a bit – proprietorial."

"You've only seen them together for a few minutes," Clare pointed out.

"True. But her kind of woman can slap a 'Booked' notice on a man by the very way she looks at him – in front of other women." Oscar glanced at his watch. "By the way, these characters are overdue. What do we do about that?"

"Wait for them, I suppose. Frank may have got lost again," Clare suggested.

"If so, he has only to ask. He's got a tongue in his head."

"Not an Italian tongue. But if that's all that's the matter, they can't be long. There are only so many wrong ways you can take in this town without ultimately hitting on the right one, by the law of averages."

Clare had spoken confidently, but when they had waited for some twenty minutes longer, making more than an hour in all, she was worried and inwardly blaming herself for having agreed to the parting of company of which the others had thought nothing. Even Oscar, she supposed, was only worried now lest something had happened to his car. *He* hadn't been made responsible for Eirene as she had, and *he* hadn't been reminded, as she had been only yesterday, of just how far Tarquin considered her responsibilities went. Besides, if he had occasion to blame her today, she had to admit he would have a point. Being a party to losing Eirene on their first day out together was pretty culpable after all.

She watched Oscar doing a quarter-deck march of impatience and muttering dark threats against Frank. It wasn't until they had waited some time longer that she realised they were both pretending a little that they were merely irked, not deeply worried over the worst that the delay could mean.

Oscar came to lean on the parapet, peering into the gathering dusk. "So what's our next move?" he wanted to know.

Clare shivered. "I think you'd better stay here, and I'll go up to the Casa." She didn't want to, but there was no help for it. "Frank and Eirene may just have gone there, and even if not – "

"Yes, her people must be told," Oscar agreed. "I'll stay here in case they do turn up. Do you mind going alone?"

It wasn't the going that Clare minded; it was confessing to Eirene's family that she had no idea of the girl's whereabouts. She hated worrying the Signora and Nicola, and if Tarquin were at the Casa – !

Tarquin was not at the Casa. As Clare approached his villa she saw there were two cars outside it, Tarquin's which she recognised and a smaller sports car. She was still some way off when she saw Tarquin and Jaquetta come out and pause at the top of the steps. Their figures, in silhouette to Clare, were very close, as Jaquetta laid a hand on each of his lapels, stood on tiptoe and kissed him full on his mouth. Then she ran down one branch of the steps; he went down the other. They met at her car, where she took the driving-seat, lifted a hand to him, did a tight U-turn and sped past Clare without seeing her.

But Tarquin evidently had, for he came to meet her.

"What are you doing, walking alone?" he demanded. "Where is Eirene? And your escorts – both of them?"

CHAPTER FOUR

CLARE said, "I'm on my way to the Casa. I've left Oscar Bridgeman on Liberty Square, where we had arranged to meet his nephew and Eirene – "

"To meet them? I thought you were all together?"

"We were. But Eirene got bored and Frank Bridgeman borrowed the car to take her for a drive. That was when we split up."

"When was this?"

"A couple of hours ago, before the Pallium ended."

"You were *at* the Pallium?" To Clare his emphasis seemed to voice doubt and she flushed.

"Of course."

"I didn't see you there."

"I didn't see *you*. But Oscar Bridgeman and I were there until the end." At a sudden thought (Bless Lucio!) she added, "If you don't believe me, ask your uncle Lucio. He saw us and spoke to us."

Tarquin said, "Don't be so touchy. I don't need proof of your word. But you parted company there, and the other two went for a drive? Where to?"

"I don't know. Just for a drive round. We arranged to meet again over an hour ago, but they haven't arrived. So Oscar stayed on the Square in case they did, and I came up to the Casa to see if perhaps they went straight there."

"Why should they, if they had arranged to meet you and Bridgeman senior at the Square?"

"It was only an idea. When you begin to be – afraid, you have to think of everything."

"And you are afraid of what may have happened?"

"A bit."

He looked at her keenly. "I can see you are. You're trembling. But it's too soon to imagine the worst. Come inside for a few minutes, and I'll go to the Casa." His hand under her elbow turned her towards the steps, but she shook free.

"No, I must go – "

"And alarm Mama and Nicola, perhaps unnecessarily? If you arrive alone, they will guess there is something wrong, whereas I can look in and leave again without causing any remark. If the other two are there, there is no harm done. And if they're not, it will be time enough then to make enquiries."

Clare's heart sank. "Enquiries?"

"Get a search afoot – the police, the hospital."

"Oh – yes." This time she obeyed the urging of his hand. He opened the door on to a small square vestibule and another door into a living-room, where he gestured her to a chair and went to a drinks cabinet in a corner. He poured a small cognac into a glass, added a level of soda water and brought it to her. "Drink that. It will steady you," he said. "I'll be back very soon."

She sipped gratefully. She felt ashamed. Tarquin knew she had been a nurse, and he must wonder at her lack of control. What he couldn't know was that, expecting his censure, she had been disabled by his brusque, practical concern for her. He hadn't blamed her. He had simply taken over her problem himself, and the relief had been briefly unnerving. He ought to have been angry, and he hadn't been. He had been – kind.

She looked about her at the furnishings of the room; at the

64

open bookshelves, at the two enormous pottery floor-vases, each in its graceful alcove, at the heavy linen curtaining, at the photographs on a bureau – of the Signora, a wedding picture of Nicola and her husband, of Tarquin himself and another man, wearing their ceremonial uniform and insignia as Captains Regent, snapshots of Nicola and Jaquetta on a beach, of Jaquetta alone, of Jaquetta kneeling behind Tarquin, playfully blindfolding his eyes. Clare remembered Oscar's word "proprietorial" and thought, yes, the assurance with which Jaquetta had kissed Tarquin on parting from him just now had been all of that.

When he returned, surprisingly he brought Oscar with him. Frank and Eirene, he told Clare, had arrived safely enough at the Casa. They had variously lost their way, suffered a puncture, and made a long detour to give a lift to two farm labourers trudging home. Supposing that Oscar and Clare wouldn't have waited for them so long, they had bypassed the rendezvous and made straight for the Casa, causing no alarm there, only surprise that Oscar and Clare were not there before them. Tarquin had then collected Oscar, relieved and grateful, from the Square.

Oscar accepted the drink Tarquin offered him; Clare refused to have her glass refilled; Tarquin poured for himself and sat down, making conversation by asking Oscar what was the business he was engaged in.

Oscar told him all that he had told Clare of his circumstances and his prospects. But unlike Clare, Tarquin had some pertinent questions to ask.

He confirmed that Giovanni Fiore was Jaquetta's father, then said, "You propose to sink all your available capital in this scheme?"

"If necessary, yes," said Oscar.

"And how much of Italian business methods and legal proceedings do you understand?"

"Well – Are they so very different from English ones?" Oscar parried.

Tarquin shrugged. "You may find them so, especially if you haven't a good command of the language."

"I'm picking it up – "

"You'll need to." Tarquin's tone was dry. "And supposing you get your land, what do you know about building or property management?"

"Well, building – I shall use contractors. My idea is an estate of smallish luxury bungalows for sale and rent, and I shall be on pretty safe ground in the matter of management. That I understand. It has been part of my job."

"And I take it you are footloose – your own master?"

Oscar laughed. "So far, if by footloose you mean whether I'm engaged or married or have 'encumbrances' of any sort."

"That was what I meant," said Tarquin.

Clare and Oscar left a few minutes later, and once outside, Oscar drew an exaggerated breath. "Pff, what a grilling! You'd suppose that I'd gone to *him* for financial backing, at the very least," he grumbled. "Or had asked for his favourite sister's hand!"

"You mean all those questions to you? Well, I think he's like that. He doesn't give up until he's learnt all he wants to know," said Clare.

"Even if it's no affair of his? But he has had you at the receiving end of the same kind of inquisition?"

"Yes – once."

"I suppose when you applied for the job with Eirene? But for goodness' sake! – he's not employing *me*!"

Nor had there been any mention of employment for her when Tarquin had originally worn her down with his un-sparing questions. Then, for some reason of his own, he had forced himself into her confidence, unwillingly given. But she didn't tell Oscar so. On the defensive for Tarquin's compulsive methods (as if he needed her on his side!) she let the subject drop.

The days began to take on a pattern. The girls would breakfast with Nicola and lunch and dine *en famille* with the Signora, Nicola and the uncles, with Tarquin coming in each morning and often to a meal.

Signora Roscuro rarely went out, except with Tarquin in his car. She read, sitting ramrod-straight in a high chair, worked at *gros-point* embroidery on a frame, and "received" her friends socially – the women usually to coffee and cakes in the morning, the married ones with their husbands to the occasional dinner-party. She left the domestic management of the house to Nicola who, with Anna's help, ran it with serene efficiency. In her spare time Nicola knitted and sewed happily for her coming baby's layette, often saying amusedly of herself that she had been designed at birth as a cabbage – sturdily rooted and well bulked, and was content to be that way.

For the most part the uncles Lucio and Paolo remained sublimely aloof from the household's affairs, preoccupied with their own interests and only now and then to be drawn out about them. It appeared they were indeed twins, and in consequence were dubbed "Dum" and "Dee" by Eirene, though she didn't attempt the daunting task of explaining the reference to them.

Eirene herself, though voluble enough about most things, was not communicative about the fraught situation between her parents which had torn her up by the roots and sent her to San Marino.

She had the occasional letter from her father, whom she described to Clare as a trouble-shooter – an electronics expert, constantly abroad, advising foreign purchasers on the use of the computers they had bought from his firm. Her letters from her mother came from South Africa, where Mrs. Landor

67

had gone to stay with friends, and when either of such letters arrived, she would pocket it and presumably read it when she was alone, sharing its contents with no one. And in answer to the Signora's enquiries as to how her mother or her father were, she would volunteer only an airy "Oh, they're fine" – which, considering Mrs. Landor was Signora Roscuro's niece, Clare thought was cavalier, if not ungracious, and once ventured to say so in remonstrance to Eirene.

Eirene turned mulish. "So what – if they *are* fine?" she queried. "What else could I say?"

"I'd have thought you could pass on some of the news in your people's letters. There must be some that isn't private which your great-aunt would like to hear, surely?"

"News? What news? That Daddy has just come back from *here* and is off tomorrow to *there*? Or that the sun in Cape Town is wonderful, but that the wind never stops blowing? What is there to interest Aunt Emilia in that? Anyway, if she wants to be told any more than that, so far as they ever tell me they're well and happy, she can always ask for more, can't she?"

"Not, I'd say, if you show no sign of wanting to tell her more and just shut up like a clam."

"Or perhaps" – Eirene's tone was savage and she was frowning as Clare had seen her frown at her first sight of the Casa – "perhaps you think I ought to tell Aunt Emilia that neither of them – neither Daddy nor Mummy – ever mention each other? *Ever*! Well, do you?" she pressed.

Contrite, and shocked from censure into pity, Clare began, "Oh, Eirene, I'm sorry! I didn't realise – " only for Eirene to storm,

"Of course not. How could you? *Your* mother and father loved each other and went on doing it. You've said so. But mine have apparently stopped – just like that – " before she turned and ran, leaving Clare feeling helpless in face of a

68

problem which, pity Eirene as she might, she could do nothing about. Except sympathise and try to reassure, if Eirene would let her.

But Eirene did not let her. Not unnaturally the exchange caused a rift between them, but it lasted no longer than the time it took for Eirene's spirits to recover their buoyancy, and when Clare tried to make amends, the only response she got was Eirene's "Forget it. You couldn't have known," which didn't encourage her to say any more.

Having soon exhausted the attractions of the town's shops, Eirene began to cast about for other occupations with which to fill her time. She didn't read and she hadn't enough Italian to enjoy a visit to the cinema, and though unexpectedly, hoyden as she was, she had a flair for fine needlework and offered to add smocking and embroidery to Nicola's baby clothes, she would only work at this in the evenings when she and Clare were always at home.

Frank Bridgeman had acquired his scooter and had telephoned for permission to take Eirene out on it. But this was not encouraged by the Casa, the Signora ruling that she considered it *brutta figura* for young girls to go pillion-riding, which Nicola translated for Eirene, "Mama thinks it is bad form, and she would not like you to do it. She does not forbid it, you understand, but perhaps you will not displease her in this?"

So Eirene, equally tactfully persuaded by Clare that it was evidently "not done" in Roscuro social circles, bowed to the inevitable and invited Frank to luncheon and to swim with her and Clare at Jaquetta's invitation to her pool. The three of them walked down and back, and Frank went home at the sedate hour of five o'clock.

Clare could not have said just when she realised that Jaquetta was gradually but studiedly cultivating Eirene's acquaintance, at the same time excluding Clare herself.

It had begun with one or two casual morning calls by telephone. Jaquetta was going to take a dip, but she hated swimming alone. Would Eirene possibly care to swim too? Eirene had cared – with enthusiasm. Clare had pointed out that only she had been invited, and though Eirene demurred, "Well no, but – " she did go alone, and after the first time, usually did.

Then there were expeditions into Rimini by car – for shopping, for ices and coffee at one of the smart hotels, for a dress show for which Jaquetta had only two tickets. Such a *pity*, she apologised when she called for Eirene, that she wasn't able to take Clare along too. Just as, when she first invited Eirene to drive with her to Rimini, she had been sad that in her little sports car there was really no comfort for three . . .

Eirene, admiring Jaquetta as she did, was excusably flattered by the older girl's attentions. Moreover, she was learning quite a lot of Italian from Jaquetta, she claimed. In fact, she was even beginning to help Frank with his Italian, whenever he dropped in at the villa too.

Clare had reacted rather sharply to that. "You've been seeing Frank there since he came here to lunch?" she asked.

"Only when Jaquetta has suggested I invite him. Just for a swim in the pool, that's all."

"How often?"

Eirene shrugged. "Not so very. Once or twice. Jaquetta likes him. She thinks he's a nice friend for me, and says it isn't as if Aunt Emilia didn't know him and hadn't received him. And if they don't like my having seen him at her villa instead of here, I'll tell her and she will put it right with them."

"And I'm sure she could. All the same, I do think you should say some time – though as casually as you like – that she does invite him there, and that you've been seeing him," Clare advised.

"In case they think I'm guilty of the too, too awful 'form' of going pillion behind him, which I'm not? But all right, I'll drop a word about Frank, some time or other. When I think of it," Eirene promised.

But whether or not she "thought of it" when Clare was not present, Clare did not know. Anyway, perhaps she was being over-conscientious. Perhaps it didn't matter, and perhaps Jaquetta did know for certain that anything which found approval with her would go all the way with the Roscuros too.

Of course Clare and Eirene still did a number of things together, especially as Jaquetta's invitations tended to come in spasmodic bunches and then to drop off in favour of her other engagements. But increasingly Clare began to feel redundant to Eirene's need for companionship. Sometimes she thought wryly that if Jaquetta had deliberately set out to supplant her, she could hardly have done it better, with the effect of causing Clare to ask herself whether, in the role of Eirene's *camerata*, she was still earning her salary and her keep! And it didn't help either that when Jaquetta called for Eirene to take her somewhere or other, she would congratulate herself on being able to relieve Nicola, or Clare, of the responsibility of entertaining Eirene, murmuring to Nicola's "You are very kind, Jaquetta," a deprecatory, "No trouble at all. I like to do it. And if I did not, the child might have rather a dull time, mightn't she?" – which, to Clare's mind, effectually belittled the role for which she herself had been engaged and was being paid. But this was something which Nicola, grateful to Jaquetta, did not seem to notice, and even Tarquin merely noticed far enough as to congratulate Eirene on her increasing fluency in Italian when she had been out with Jaquetta without Clare several times.

Meanwhile Clare had her own leisure to fill. She went twice more with Lucio to the Armoury, and once Paolo volunteered that Tarquin had mentioned her interest in the Roscuro family tree. If she would like to see his drawing up of the full one, he would gladly show it to her, he said.

71

It was a most impressive document and clearly a loving life's work. It was hand-printed in Paolo's beautiful script and housed in a cabinet in rolled sections which took a whole afternoon for him to display to Clare. It must have taken him years to amass the data and do the research for it – lives, marriages, births, deaths; all but the currently living Roscuros reduced to names and dates, and occupations wherever Paolo had been able to trace these latter.

As he rolled up the last one, with the Casa Torre branch of the family showing Nicola's marriage to Marco Bernini as the latest item, he answered the unspoken question which delicacy prevented Clare's putting to him.

"You are wondering," he said, "what will become of it when I am gone?"

"Well, I – "

His smile twinkled. "But of course this is what you were asking yourself about an old man's hobby! Well, I trust I shall be spared to enter up at least the first of Nicola's children, and Tarquin's marriage and *his* firstborn and more. But if I'm not, and when I do die, I can safely leave this record to Tarquin to carry on. For he has reverence for the family, and cares about it. And that is the best thing about 'family', as we Latins well know – that there is always someone – or more than one – on whom it is possible to rely, as upon nobody else in the world. Do you not agree, *signorina*?"

But Clare thought of the Cavours, and the resulting revolt of spirit they had caused her. "I think it must depend on the kind of family," she demurred. "Some aren't at all close; some too close; some jealous and hard; some – "

Paolo shook his head, rejecting that. "No," he said firmly. "In every family there is good to be found, if you look for it. And in every family there is enough of all that matters for everyone – work, and play, and love. Or so we Italians believe. And what can anyone ask more of life than these?"

Clare gave in, faced by a question which obviously his faith saw as unanswerable, with all those centuries of family-linked Roscuros and, on his side, of Marinis behind him. She allowed her murmured agreement with him to end the argument, and as she left him she found she was thinking that, with that length of recorded line behind her, she would like her own name to be written into just such a chart for the people who came after her to point to and say "I remember her" or "Who was she?" Later still she was remembering the most unimportant of detail about the Roscuros' current chart the line already ruled below the Berninis' names, ready for their children's, and the = sign beside Tarquin's name, ready for his wife's name to follow.

Did Tarquin know what entry he meant Paolo should make there? she wondered. Had Oscar Bridgeman's rather cynical guess been right, and it would be Jaquetta Fiore's? Or if not hers, then whose?

Evidently it was a question which Eirene had also pondered, without knowing the answer. "Do you suppose Tarquin and Jaquetta are unofficially engaged?" she queried of Clare one day. "He doesn't seem to take any other woman about alone as he does her. But she doesn't wear a ring, so I wondered."

"Hasn't she confided in you whether they are or not?" asked Clare.

"She hints at it sometimes, but I don't think there's anything definite. Anyway, fancy marrying into this family! You wouldn't just be taking on a man, but a dynasty, no less. Have you *seen* that chart hanging in the hall? It goes back to the year dot and beyond!"

"I've also seen the whole family tree," said Clare. "Your uncle Paolo showed it to me – main stem, branches, twigs, the lot."

"Am I on it?" asked Eirene, interested.

"You're on the Marini one, the first link of that with the

Roscuros being your great-aunt's marriage to Tarquin's and Nicola's father. It isn't as detailed a line, anyway, as the Roscuro one. Your uncle hasn't been able to trace it back as far as theirs."

"No? Too bad about that," mocked Eirene lightly. Then she drew her shoulders together and shivered. "Ugh! Fancy one day being just a name on a fusty bit of parchment that's kept in a glass case or framed. Doesn't bear thinking about, does it?"

"Then don't think about it," Clare advised. "But your name is there on the Marini chart, whether you like it or not."

It was on an afternoon when Eirene was again out with Jaquetta, and Nicola and the Signora were resting, that Tarquin came into the *salotto* where Clare was doing an Italian exercise from a book she had bought in the town.

He looked over her shoulder. "Taking your Italian seriously? Where is Eirene?" he asked.

"Signorina Fiore has taken her to an English film in Rimini."

"You didn't want to go too?"

"I – I'd already seen it," she lied.

"Oh. Well, I'd thought of taking you both on a tour of the kilns. But if you'd care to come along alone, I can take her another time. You'd be interested, I daresay?"

In the car he explained that though it was usual to speak of "the kilns" the term included the whole of the Roscuro ceramics plant—the clay pits, the sandstone quarries, the pottery block, the design studios, the engraving shops, as well as the executive offices and the despatch warehouses. It occupied an immense area at the edge of the town and employed hundreds of people. "We have some who are the fifth and sixth generations of their families who have been in ceramics," he told Clare.

He proved a meticulous guide, showing her first the modern

offices, humming with activity. Then he said, "We'll take it backwards, I think – the end-product first and from there to where it all begins," and led the way to the big gallery where masses of ornamental jars, vases, plaques and carvings were gathered on tables, ready for despatch.

The pottery was of all shapes – some classically curved and voluted, some squat and functional and as modern as tomorrow. The classical ones depended mainly on line for their appeal; the moderns wore designs of the liveliest colours, mostly in relief. There was a special gathering of mugs, plates, vases, cruets in readiness for the next season's tourist trade – all showing the San Marino coat-of-arms and either the Basilica or the Parliament House or one or other of the three Towers.

When Tarquin asked Clare her preference in the different types she rejected these latter. "On the whole, they're rather gaudy," she said.

"You think so? They sell well. People buy them by the hundred as mementoes of their visits here. They are standard lines that are never allowed to run out of stock," Tarquin remarked.

"Yes, well – once having seen San Marino, I don't think I'd ever need a reminder of it."

"Wouldn't need one, or wouldn't want one?"

"Wouldn't need one in the shape, say, of a coffee-pot or a wall-plate. When I leave here I think I shall want to remember it for the way I've seen it myself – in sharp sunshine or after the sun has gone down or on a windy day when the clouds go racing past. Or, of course, by moonlight – "

"You feel the charm of the place, then?"

"I envy you it," she said simply. She moved over to a table of vases of classical design, with a shelf above on which only three or four pieces were displayed. She touched a gracefully-handled one. "I like this," she said. "Oh – and *that*!" pointing to the shelf.

Tarquin laughed shortly as he took down the vase and put it into her hands. "You've certainly got taste," he said. "These are the very few unique pieces we do – unique in that only one of each shape and design is made. You couldn't buy a pair of any of them if you tried, and they are never repeated."

"This is lovely." Clare's finger traced the swelling line from base to neck and turned the vase to admire its only decoration – a trailing stem and leaves of acanthus in very light relief in self-colour, a cream that was almost translucent. She handed it back and Tarquin replaced it without comment. On their way out he picked up a squat coffee mug in either hand and offered them to her. "You're sure you don't prefer these?"

Round the base of one trailed a procession of grotesque cats; the other showed a somewhat Cubist priest on a bicycle, and Clare shuddered. "No indeed!" she said.

"They're the latest 'with-it' thing. You're a reactionary!" he accused her.

She nodded. "Though what is so wrong about that?"

"Nothing. At heart I'm one myself, but in business one has to remember that one man's meat is another's poison, and that it takes all sorts – " he said carelessly, unaware, she knew, of her little ripple of pleasure at his agreement with her.

They went next to the painting and engraving rooms, where rows of girls painted by hand with swift, sure strokes and there was a steady buzz from the men's engraving wheels. From there to the pottery shops and the smooth, skilled caressing of the raw clay up and up, into the body curves of bowls and the slender necks of vases and the squat fatness and generous mouths of mugs. And so, finally, to the open yards where the clay was stored and kept moist and where the rough stone of the quarries was piled in small mountains, untouched as yet by mallet or chisel.

Except that it was here, Tarquin said, that the apprentice masons practised the first use of their tools, and pointed to a

76

group of teenage boys who were chipping away at shapeless blocks of stone on a nearby bench.

"We all have to begin here. I did myself," he told Clare, and they stood watching until a man approached him to say that he was wanted on the phone in his office.

"Coming," he said, and to Clare, "Will you come, or wait for me, and I'll come back?" and nodded when she elected to stay.

There seemed to be no foreman around and as soon as Tarquin had left the boys began to idle and lark about, cat-calling and jostling and hurling tools like javelins from one to the other. It was some minutes before Clare realised that a lot of the showing-off was aimed at her notice, but when she did she decided it was probably time she left before the horseplay turned to havoc. But as she turned away, she halted, her blood curdling at the savage, almost animal howl of pain which went up behind her.

She turned back. The rollicking had stopped and the boys had grouped, shouting alarm, around one who was bent double, clutching his wrist at knee-level. As Clare darted forward his knees buckled and he sank to the floor, still grasping the wrist, and she saw the bright blood which spurted from the jagged tear in the flesh.

Someone picked up and brandished the chisel which must have caused the wound; the boy rocked his head from side to side; the frenzied, unhelpful jabbering went on, and as Clare thrust people aside to kneel by the boy an older man appeared and began to ask rough, staccato questions which no one answered coherently.

Compressing the wound with her fingers, Clare looked up at him. "*Lei e il capofabbrica?*" she asked, gratified that she knew the Italian for "foreman".

"*Si, si, signora.*"

"And you have bandages?" she demonstrated in mime.

77

"*Si, si.*" His jerked thumb sent a boy for the first-aid cabinet.

"There is a nurse? A doctor?"

He shook his head. "Not here. At the hospital – both," he said, surprising Clare, who though she hadn't expected a resident doctor, certainly thought a plant of this size would employ an industrial nurse.

"Well, I am a nurse," she said, selecting lint and bandages from the box and setting to on the essential job of staunching the blood. When she had finished she stood and helped the boy up, an arm round his shoulders. "He must go to the hospital," she told the foreman. "Can you see to that?"

But before he could answer Tarquin was there, his glance going from the drooping boy to Clare's bloodstained dress and asking, "What?"

The foreman broke into a voluble tirade; the boys fell back and tried to look busy, and Clare explained, "His wrist is rather badly cut – by a chisel, I think. So I've given him first aid, but he ought to have it properly treated and stitched in hospital."

"Yes, of course. Bring him to the sick bay, will you, and I'll ring for a taxi from there. You too," Tarquin added to the foreman. "I'll be sending you with him, and you can wait and take him home if they don't want to keep him overnight."

The clinic and the sick bay were so well equipped that Clare, finding it difficult to believe it wasn't attended by a nurse, questioned Tarquin about it when they had returned to his office after despatching the boy by taxi.

"But of course we employ one full-time," he said. "It so happens, though, that she went on a fortnight's leave yesterday, leaving us dependent on the State nurse, who visits us twice a day and whom we can call on in an emergency. Vascello should have told you."

"I'm afraid my Italian wasn't getting through to him very well. And anyway, there was no time to waste."

"And it seems none was, thanks to you. Supposing you hadn't been there, or hadn't known how to cope? We have to be very grateful to you, you know."

She flushed at the praise. "It was nothing. I *was* there and I *could* cope. And if I hadn't, I daresay somebody – "

"You were there when it happened? You saw it all?"

"Yes. After you left the boys started scuffling and throwing things. It was a chisel that did it, I think, but it was a pure accident."

"Wasn't Vascello there?"

"Not until after it happened – " Clare broke off as the telephone rang. Tarquin lifted the receiver and gave his number.

After a minute or two he said, "I'm sorry about that. What have you done with it?" and listened again.

"And so?" he queried. And then, "I'm afraid I can't, straight away. I have Clare here with me, and I'm taking her home. What's that? Yes – Clare; Clare Yorke. You'd better take a taxi – " He paused and listened. Then, "Very well, if you are prepared to wait and will say where you will be, I'll come down later."

Replacing the receiver, he told Clare, "That was Jaquetta Fiore in trouble with her car in the city. She says it is raining, and all the taxis are taken, so I've said I'll go down and fetch her and Eirene later, after I've driven you home. Are you ready to come now?"

Making conversation in the car, he asked, "When the surgeons say you may, do you mean to go back to nursing?"

"Oh yes. I want to finish my training and qualify. After all, it's the only thing I know."

"The only thing? You've adapted well enough here, haven't you?"

"Thank you. But I meant nursing is the only skilled job I know."

"Though you would have given it up for marriage?"

"It had given me up by the time I met Bruno Cavour, and we probably should never have met if I'd still been working," Clare pointed out.

"You could have met someone else, and you'll meet other men, one or other of whom may pass your acid test — of his needing to be a lone wolf, with no other loyalties hampering his courtship of you, I mean."

She flinched. "I suppose I deserved that."

"Only if you are of the same biased views as you were when we first met. But if you've decided to widen the young men's chances, then naturally I wish them happy hunting — and you, all you hope of marriage when it happens for you."

"Thank you," she said again. *But how I wish I could think you really cared whether or not I've lived down that piece of bitterness!* The words had formed so clearly in her mind that she could almost believe she had spoken them. But of course she had not, nor would. That she badly wanted him to think better of her in this and to hear him say so, wasn't for telling to him. Nor must she let him guess at her sudden disturbing need to have his good will in everything, in every way. For when he withheld it, that was to ask again to be hurt. And when he gave it, that was to glow too much.

When they reached the Casa he helped her out. "Thank you again for this afternoon," he said.

She smiled. "I've told you, I just happened to be there!"

"I wasn't only referring to your first aid." He got back into the car and she watched him turn it and drive away at the bidding of Jaquetta Fiore, from whom she supposed she could be said to have had the loan of him for the afternoon.

But he had implied that he had enjoyed her company, and the glow was there.

CHAPTER FIVE

THAT evening Eirene told Clare casually, "I think Jaquetta does regard Tarquin as her property, because until he told her on the way home that he had only been showing you round the kilns, she seemed quite put out that you were with him when she rang up."

"Why should she mind?" Clare queried.

"I don't know. But after she had telephoned she seemed rather peeved that he was making us wait to be collected, and she said she had needed to question who 'Clare' was. She had forgotten for the moment it was you, and anyway she hadn't realised that you and Tarquin were on first-name terms. So of course I told her that was my idea – that for any of us here to go on calling you Miss Yorke made you sound like a governess in horn-rims and a shirt-blouse and brown brogues, which you're not," claimed Eirene.

"*Only* in spectacles, a shirt-blouse and brogues, I'd be in danger of being arrested," Clare teased. "What did Jaquetta say to that?"

"Nothing really. Just that it was her mistake – a kind of governess to me being what she understood you were. And then she asked whether you were still seeing or hearing from Oscar Bridgeman. So I told her we had met in Rimini two or three times – the four of us."

"And Oscar rang up the other day when you were out,"

Clare said. "Tarquin was here and took the call and told me it was Oscar, asking for me. It was only to say that his land purchase – from the Fiore firm, by the way – was on the point of going through, and that when it did, he hoped we could celebrate somehow."

"Just you and Oscar, or Frank and me as well?" asked Eirene hopefully.

"Oh, I'm sure he meant a foursome," Clare assured her. "There would be no point in his asking just me to celebrate a deal which is going to involve Frank as well. Anyway, he's going to call me again when it's really settled, and we can see what he suggests then."

But Oscar had not rung again in the matter of his land deal by the time the next big event in the San Marino calendar came up – the installation of that autumn's newly-elected Captains Regent, which occasioned another day of fête and junketings for the town.

As for the lesser Pallium contest, the shops were closed, the streets were again beflagged and everyone turned out for the solemnity of the ceremony at which the Captains-elect – in their traditional fifteenth-century elegance of silk corselet, knee breeches, black velvet capes and ermine-edged beret – accepted the homage of the retiring Captains, attended by the Army in full dress uniform, the State judges, the Councillors, the Diplomatic Corps and the Church. Once the new Captains were installed and invested with the regalia of their office, they became, as Tarquin had told Clare, the equal of the world's Royalties and Presidents for the period of their reign.

It was an occasion for gaiety which the holiday mood of the Sammarinese did not attempt to resist. The Roscuros could have accepted invitations in triplicate to drinks parties, musical soirées or carnival masques, had they wished. But Jaquetta had put in an early claim to their company at the restaurant party she was giving at a hotel in Rimini, rejecting any of those in San Marino on the score that they would be crowded to their doors.

The Signora had excused herself with grace. The uncles took it for granted that they were not expected to accept. Nicola wanted to demur that as a grass widow she would be *de trop* – a plea which Jaquetta demolished by saying that her father, as a real widower, would also be without a partner if Nicola wouldn't honour him. So the party from the Casa Torre would comprise Tarquin, Nicola, Eirene and Clare – Clare's invitation having come to her via Eirene, along with the news that Jaquetta had asked Frank Bridgeman for Eirene and Oscar for Clare. No one doubted of course that Jaquetta was arranging for Tarquin to partner her.

Oscar did ring up on the day before the party, not to say that his deal had been finalised but to ask if he might drive up for Clare the following evening.

"Well, I don't know–" She hadn't heard what arrangements Tarquin had made for their transport, but as she hesitated, he came in at the front door, and she put a hand over the mouthpiece.

"It's Oscar Bridgeman," she told him.

"Wanting?"

"Offering to call for me and drive me down to Rimini to-morrow night. He means Eirene too, I suppose."

"Then thank him, but tell him I shall be taking the three of you in my car," said Tarquin. "You and Eirene can meet him and his nephew at the restaurant."

"Oh – " Clare kept her hand over the mouthpiece and noticing this, Tarquin questioned, "Well?"

"Well, he sounded as if he thought he ought to escort us all the way."

"And I'd rather he didn't. I've seen his car; you and Eirene and Nicola will be in evening things, and mine is much more suitable."

"Very well, I'll tell him," Clare said, and did so as tactfully as she could.

A week before the party the Signora had made the auntly gesture to Eirene of telling her to buy a new dress for the occasion and to debit the cost to her. And to Clare's utter surprise she did the same for her, brushing aside Clare's embarrassed thanks by saying regally, "Jaquetta's party is an occasion for you young people, and you must do her credit by appearing at your prettiest and best."

So Eirene and Clare had gone shopping together, and however subtly Jaquetta had usurped her own role as Eirene's companion, Clare had to admit that she had improved Eirene's bizarre taste in clothes. Jaquetta always dressed exquisitely, whatever she wore appearing exactly right for informal or formal occasions alike, and Clare felt that something of her flair had rubbed off on Eirene when she turned her back on the garish colours and accessories she would have chosen a month or earlier, favouring instead an almost demure princess-line dress in buttercup yellow without a superfluous frill or flounce about it to spoil its simple effect. She was wearing her hair longer too – long enough to afford her some choice of style whenever she troubled to do more than pull a comb through its everyday porcupine quills and secure it with a forehead band worn just above her eyebrows. On the afternoon of the party, she told Clare, Jaquetta's own hairdresser was going to style it for her. Jaquetta would be taking her to the salon, but why didn't Clare ring up and make an appointment to have her own hair done too?

Clare made one. It was for a rather later time than Eirene's, so she did not go with them when Jaquetta called for Eirene to keep hers. And on arriving at the salon Clare was a little too early for her own, the receptionist apologised. They were very busy and somewhat behindhand, but if the *signora* would take a seat, she should not be kept waiting long.

"The *signora*" took a seat in the rosy-hued, scented waiting-room where, coming in out of the sharp sunlight, she had to adjust to its soft lighting before she saw that its only other occupant was Jaquetta, waiting too.

At sight of Clare, Jaquetta flipped shut the glossy magazine she had been reading. "I'm waiting to collect Eirene," she explained. "It's unusual for Bonita not to keep her appointments to the exact minute of starting and finishing, but I insisted she should attend Eirene herself, as she does me, of course, and I'm prepared to forgive her for keeping me waiting if she does what I hope she may with the child's hair."

Clare murmured politely, "I know Eirene was delighted that you suggested Bonita should do it."

"And so she should be," said Jaquetta practically. "Bonita is more than a hairdresser, she is an artist, the equal of any man. But very expensive." Jaquetta paused. "Are you a regular client of hers yourself? I shouldn't have thought – "

The smooth implication that she had no right to patronise Jaquetta's own expensive hairdresser made Clare's hackles rise. But still polite, she laughed. "Not very often. In fact, this is the first time," she admitted.

"Ah, then I don't expect you will get Bonita. But her assistants are mostly very good," Jaquetta conceded. "But where else have you been, since you have been in San Marino?"

"Nowhere, except for cutting. I can usually manage it myself."

"Really? How clever of you." Jaquetta's glance studied the smooth fall of Clare's hair for a minute. "And I suppose, now that I'm able to give Eirene a rather better time than she might have had otherwise, you find your own time much less occupied than you had expected?"

"So that I have leisure enough for doing my own hair, you mean?" Clare queried.

"And for other things. In fact, I've sometimes joked to Eirene that she ought to spend less time with me and more with you, lest you should begin to feel that you are rather too under-employed for safety."

"For *safety*?" Clare echoed.

"The safety of your job, I meant. After all, you *were* engaged to keep Eirene company and from being bored, which she never is with me, and if the Roscuros did decide you were a little redundant now, they might – " Jaquetta broke off and amended, "not that the Signora and Nicola aren't far too kind to wish to go back on any contract they have made with you. But Tarquin, in my experience, is just a little ruthless about discarding anything or anyone he has not further use for – " She stood up, extending both hands in a theatrical gesture to Eirene who was emerging from a nearby cubicle.

"Eirene, *carita*! How charming! All I had hoped for you!" Jaquetta turned to the woman in a rose-pink uniform who had followed Eirene out. "Bonita, you are a genius! You have transformed her – as if I didn't know you could!"

Bonita smiled. "You approve, Signorina Fiore?"

"*Approve?* It is a magic. And you, child, you like yourself too?"

Ignoring Clare, they stood over Eirene, self-conscious but extraordinarily pretty and newly groomed, her hair a smooth brown cap for her head, pointed to her nape, and ends turning piquantly upward on her cheeks, and the front trained to a Florentine curve across her brow. Seeing Clare, she came over. "New Look Eirene," she dimpled. "What's the verdict?"

Clare gave it in a double thumbs-up sign. "Super," she said, her response to Eirene's obvious pleasure for the moment allaying the sting of Jaquetta's so-casually barbed comment which Eirene's arrival had cut short. Though she didn't her-self doubt that once Tarquin saw her as dispensable he

86

wouldn't make a charity of keeping her in idleness, it irked her to be told as much in so many words. It rankled all through her own session with one of Bonita's minions, and if there had been any polite way of declining Jaquetta's hospitality, she thought she would be tempted to take it. But to do so at this hour would be to incommode too many people; she didn't know why Jaquetta should make her the target for her subtle slights, but since there was no way of answering back without giving offence to the Roscuros, Clare had to hold the fire of the retorts she might have made, had she been a free agent.

For her own hair she had chosen a winged, upswept style which she carried away carefully in a taxi, not daring to subject it to the capricious onslaught of the *garbino*, San Marino's own particular south wind. For her dress she wore green, shot with silver lurex thread. The draped neckline fell behind as a pointed cowl which she could draw hoodlike over her hair or leave upon her back, complementing a similar draping at her waist. Nicola, whose pregnancy was adding bloom to her features and a raven gloss to her hair, was sunnily serene in figure-hiding brown velvet, and they were all summoned to an "audience" of the Signora for her approval when they were dressed.

As usual, Nicola preferred the back seat of the car; Eirene joined her there and Clare sat beside Tarquin. After getting in she had thrown back her hood, and she was aware of his quick glance her way in appraisal of the different look of her head.

He commented, "You girls with long hair certainly have an advantage. Given a few hairpins and a comb or two and you can achieve maturity at a stroke."

She touched her hair self-consciously and laughed. "I'm afraid mine is a rather precarious maturity, achieved with more pins than I'd care to admit," she said.

"It still becomes you," he said, as Eirene, overhearing, sat forward to demand, "What about me? Aren't I transformed too?"

"You? You're just reasonably neat – for a change," he told her over his shoulder, ignoring her grimace and the "Beast!" she muttered in his ear.

When they arrived at the restaurant she and Clare were at once claimed by Frank and Oscar, while Tarquin and Nicola went to join Jaquetta and her father.

The party was to dine at separate tables in an L of the main restaurant, and when Jaquetta had greeted her guests, telling them there would be dancing in a private salon later, they took the places allotted to them by way of name-cards for the ladies, with a camellia pinned to each.

Oscar and Clare were at a table on the fringe of Jaquetta's reserved L, adjacent to the main area of tables available to other people. Their partners at the table were an older man and woman; Nicola and Signor Fiore were not far away; Frank and Eirene waved to them from a corner; Jaquetta and Tarquin were seated centrally, at the heart, as it were, of Jaquetta's guests.

Both Clare and Oscar had by now acquired enough Italian to be able to chat superficially to strangers, and their table companions were eager enough to air their own sparse English to make conversation with them pleasant and reasonably easy. The menu was excellent and the choice of wines wide; relaxed in Oscar's equable company Clare forgot her rancour against their hostess and was looking forward to whatever the rest of the evening promised. But in a pause in the talk when she was looking about her her attention was caught by the sight of a man who was passing by on the main floor of the room. He was not unsteady on his feet, but he was walking with the rather deliberate gait of the slightly drunk; he was in profile to her, but something about his build was familiar, and at a point level with her table, as if unconsciously drawn by her stare, he turned his head and looked straight at her, his loose mouth widening in a slow smile of recognition.

It was Florio Marciano. Clare drew a sharp breath, turned her back on him and hitched her chair a fraction closer to the table. The waiter was at her right hand, replenishing her wineglass, but a moment later Florio was beside him, behind her, poking three fingers hard into her shoulder.

There was nothing for it. She had to look up and round, aware of her companions' stir of puzzled interest as she met the insolent leer which went from her to them and back again. Nodding to her, he said thickly, "Well, well! You *have* found the soft places in the best of company, haven't you, little one? Done better for yourself than you might have done with poor Bruno, who found out in time what you were worth – h'm?" And then to the other three at the table: "How much do you know about this little lady, I wonder? All *I* know is that, if luck hadn't been with me, I might have had her for a sister-in-law – a loose one who isn't above spending the night with another than her affianced man – "

But he got no further. Oscar, body taut, fists ready, was on his feet, and in the next instant havoc was being wrought. The waiter, taken by surprise, stepped aside too late and dropped the bottle in his hand; Oscar's knee caught the table which tipped, causing china and glass to slide; someone at a nearby table screamed; Oscar's hard fist smashed into Florio's chin, and Florio, arms flailing wildly, went backward on his heels to collapse and double up against the knees of the lady who had screamed.

The pandemonium grew worse. The waiter, a true Latin, was talking excitedly with his hands as well as his voice and pointing to the pool of food and broken glass and crockery on the floor; Florio's unwilling prop withdrew her support from him, whereupon he knelt, then dragged himself to his feet, rocking and muttering and nursing his jaw. Feeling colour drain from her face, and as if the blood had deserted her limbs, Clare stood, shaking uncontrollably as Oscar's arm went round her shoulders, holding her up, while people talked and asked questions of each other, and Clare's one bewildered glance around her caught sight of Nicola's vexed and puzzled face across the distance between them. She would have given anything not to upset Nicola, but it seemed she had.

Then the head waiter was there, bustling his subordinate away, apologising all round, calling up lesser slaves to fetch brooms and fresh table linen and appointments and obviously gratified to give Florio Marciano into the charge of his own superior, the restaurant manager.

A trenchant word or two from the latter, and Florio slunk away, still muttering. Clare looked about her again, saw Jaquetta and Tarquin both standing by their table; Jaquetta was frowning and beating a tattoo with long, graceful fingers; Tarquin spoke to her and she nodded, and then he threaded his way to the scene of the fracas where, his face thunderous, he addressed Clare.

"What happened? Who was that man?" he demanded.

She made to shrug free of Oscar's protective arm, but he held fast. "Marciano," she told Tarquin. "Florio Marciano," and saw from his lifted brows that he had remembered the name and knew whom she meant.

"And he accosted you? What did he want?"

But she hadn't to answer that. Oscar did. "Want?" he echoed, adding in emphatic English, "The skunk came over and insulted her. *I* didn't know who he was – not a clue. But I wasn't having that, so I hit him – "

"You thought it necessary to hit him?"

"And ask questions afterwards? Of course! A drip chooses to insult your girl, what else?"

"Making a brawl, when you are a guest at a lady's party? Not exactly civilized of you, would you say?"

Oscar shrugged. "Well, of course I'm sorry about that – "

"As you should be, and I daresay you'll be apologising to Signorina Fiore. After all, there are ways of dealing with a muddled-headed drunk other than hitting him for six. You could have called the head waiter and had him slung out. That's what had to happen in the end, hadn't it?"

Oscar compressed his lips and nodded. "Except that he wasn't very drunk," he said. "I don't hit a man when he's so far sozzled that he can't defend himself. He was walking straight enough until I hit him and he knew how to choose his words to make those filthy insinuations against Clare. No, I'd give him a taste of the same any time. So if he values the rest of his ugly mug, he'd better watch out for the next chance I get to have a go at it."

"Which chance I'd advise you to forget," cautioned Tarquin. "I know the man now, and as Clare's employer, I'll see that he doesn't annoy her again in the same way."

" 'In the same way?' You weren't here. You didn't hear the mud he slung at her!" Oscar accused.

His eyes on Clare, Tarquin said evenly, "I tell you I know him, and I can guess."

Oscar glanced from Clare to him. "You – ?" he began as Tarquin went on, "Meanwhile, it would be a courtesy if you apologized to your hostess, don't you think?"

Oscar did not move. "In a minute," he said, then asked Clare, "Better now? What do you want to do?"

"I – I'd like to leave, I think. To go home." From here, where she had been shamed in sight of so many strangers, the Casa appeared as a refuge, a place where she could hide.

"Then I'll take you." Oscar looked at Tarquin. "With your permission of course, and if the Signorina will excuse her?"

Tarquin inclined his head. "If that's what she wants," he agreed.

"Then will you get your things and I'll meet you in the

foyer when I've seen Signorina Fiore?" Oscar asked, and Clare moved away, miserably over-conscious of the curious looks which she felt must be following her.

It was an impression which Oscar, solicitous for her, did his best to dispel when he rejoined her and tucked his arm in hers to show her to his car. Apologising that it had no heater, he tucked her in with a rug and consoled her, "It was a nine-minute wonder, that was all. Before I left, after being graciously forgiven by La Fiore, they were all feeding their faces again and forgetting you."

"I'm afraid Nicola Roscuro was hurt that it happened," Clare murmured. "Signora Roscuro isn't going to understand either. They do set such store here by what they call 'bella figura' – good form."

"Pff! A storm in a teacup," Oscar scoffed. "And the teacup stirred, if I may say so, by your respected employer. Also, if I may say so, he showed a good deal less concern for you than for the effect on the Signorina's guests and on the party in general."

"Well, it was an embarrassing thing to happen," Clare admitted, and then, aware of the implied criticism of him, added quickly, "But I'm terribly grateful myself. It was more than good of you to – to champion me so."

He laid a hand briefly on her rug-covered knee. "Think nothing of it," he said. "As I told Roscuro – any time, any place, I'd do the same and be glad to – for you."

"Thank you. And I mean that," she assured him.

"I'm glad." He drove in silence for some time, then said diffidently, "Care to put me in the picture? Or not? Just as you say."

"I'd better, I think. I should have told you before."

"Roscuro knows all about it, he says?"

"Yes. It was how we met."

"And – ? But no, we missed the after-dinner coffee that

92

was due to us, and there's a little *trattoria* ahead. Would you be willing to stop there, and tell me over a *cappuccino* or an ice?"

"A *cappuccino*, please."

At that hour the wayside café was empty of clients. They sat at a lino-covered table, under the indifferent eye of the proprietress, and Clare, wishing she could do the same for the ice inside her, warmed both hands by clasping them round her coffee-cup.

She began, "When we talked on Liberty Square after the Pallium I told you about the Cavours, but not the whole story. I was too ashamed of it. But it wasn't – *really !* – as that awful man claimed. I didn't – That is, I was tricked. *He* tricked me, and I – "

Oscar reached for her hand and squeezed it. "Take it easy," he advised.

"Yes, well – " With an effort, she made a brief coherent account of her escape from the intrigue against her, concluding, "That was the way it really was. You believe me, don't you?"

"If only because you could hardly make up a tale like that, and because of the kind of girl you are," Oscar assured her. He paused. "I called you 'my' girl to Roscuro. Did you notice? Did you mind?"

She evaded the question. "I don't suppose Tarquin thought you meant more by it than that you were partnering me for the evening," she said.

"Need it matter what he thought, and supposing I did mean more?" Oscar countered.

She shook her head. "You didn't. You couldn't have. The once or twice we've met for coffee, we've always been with Eirene and Frank; we've never been alone together or – talked since the Pallium."

"Well, we're alone now and we're talking now. But do you mean I'm not even to think of you as my girl, and to hope a bit?"

"I'd rather you didn't."

"Why not? Did Roscuro write 'No followers' into your contract?"

She had to smile. "Of course not."

"Then haven't you yet got over that Cavour fellow who let you down?"

"It isn't that. I've forgotten him, but – "

Oscar was waiting, and she had to go on. "Well, it's not as simple as that. I mean," she was fumbling for words, "a – a negative doesn't necessarily presuppose a positive. That I'm not in love with Bruno Cavour – if I ever were – doesn't mean that I'm ready or even want to be – serious about another man yet."

"For 'another man' read me?"

"You or – anyone. I – I'm sorry, Oscar."

"In other words, you're in a kind of emotional vacuum?"

"You could put it that way, I suppose."

"But you won't always be in it. You're dormant now, but you'll begin some time to look, and want, and feel you could love again and be loved. You will, you know. You're good and straight and honest, but you're no nun. So until – or even only in case – you do wake up, may I stick around – stay in the picture?"

She said sincerely, "I'd hate to think that I wasn't to see you any more."

He sat back in his chair, squaring his shoulders. "Fair enough," he said. "And who knows how many of those Great Romances of the world may have had to begin on less?"

He sounded satisfied, filling Clare with guilt that he should have accepted her evasions at their face value, and actually helped her to define a position she wasn't really in. For she *was* again awake to love ... did feel ... did want ... did hunger. But not for him, nor for love as love. For – !

She glanced apprehensively at Oscar, fearful lest the truth

she had admitted to herself might be written in the expression of her face. But he was smiling at her, being kind; modestly confident that they could go on from there into intimacies and closenesses for which her devious pleading may have encouraged him to hope.

She had lied to him. But what else could she have done? If he had told him there was another man for her, he would have the right to ask Who? and she couldn't have *borne* his pity and his sympathy if she had told him!

The café had had no other customers since themselves, and they left when the proprietress began an ostentatious wiping of counters and stacking of chairs. To Clare's relief Oscar was willing to discuss other things when they were in the car, and she reminded him of his promise to let her know when his land deal went through.

" 'Twixt cup and lip'," he quoted wryly. "There's always a hitch somewhere near the end, but my solicitors are coping, and it could be any day now. When we celebrate, I'll take you out to see the site. It's inland from the city, wooded and secluded and ideal for my purpose, I think."

When they reached the Casa he got out of the car with her. "Will there be anyone to let you in at this hour?" he asked.

"I think Anna, the housekeeper, may still be up. Signora Roscuro and her brothers may not be. I hope they aren't, so that I can go straight to bed. I'm sorry about tonight, Oscar. This will have spoilt your evening," she added.

"Not it," he denied. "It's done more for me than you can guess." He took both her hands and drew her closer. "But it's not quite fair, you know, to judge whether a man attracts you or not until you've given him the chance of – *this*."

She had known when his arms went round her that he meant to kiss her, and she did not resist. Her lips were warm and responsive and her body yielding while he held her. But she was cheating him. Her brief surrender was not to him, but to the fantasy that she was in another man's urgent embrace, that the kisses were his, not Oscar's – and she flung violently free, hands cupped about her burning cheeks.

Oscar stood back. "That wasn't just goodnight," he said thickly.

"I know."

"And you see what I meant?"

"Yes, but – " She stopped, ashamed.

He let her off. "I'm glad. I had to say it that way. But this *is* goodnight" – his lips touched her cheek – "and I may ring you?"

She nodded. "Please do."

He waited until Anna had opened the door to her. She fended off Anna's surprise at her early return and the offer of a hot drink. All she wanted was the refuge of her little turret room, where she could be alone to wrestle with shame and guilt and the bewilderment of loving a man who could have no suspicion of her feelings; who could judge harshly and show anger, as he had tonight; who had been generous of the time and thought he had given her more than once; who was always dynamic, a potent force in his world, where she was only a minor figure, and that for no longer than he and his family would have use for her.

Sitting on her bed, supported by her outstretched hands behind her, she said his name aloud. Tarquin. Tarquin Roscuro. Tarquin for whom she was a female presence, a voice he knew, a figure he recognised, no more than that. Tarquin who had never spoken to her nor touched her in affection, but to whom, tonight, her need had surrendered, responding to him, kiss for kiss, in the shape of Oscar, who did want her and meant that she should know it.

She had lied to Oscar and then cheated him. Just how far was it possible to sink? What could she say to him when he was next in touch? And what, tomorrow, to the Signora and

96

kind Nicola and curious Eirene? And to Tarquin, who had seemed to blame her equally with Oscar for the unruly scene Oscar had caused? And to Jaquetta, to whom she must apologise – for Tarquin would expect it.

She looked at her watch, counting the few hours of reprieve left to her. Then wearily she undressed, praying she would sleep.

Sleep, however, eluded her until about an hour before the winter dawn.

She had lain awake, listening for Nicola's and Eirene's return, wondering whether either of them would come into her. But they did not, and she was dressed and ready to go down to breakfast when Eirene knocked at her door and came to sit on her bed.

"Nicola said not to disturb you last night," she announced. "But I'm dying to know what that awful lout said to you which made Oscar knock him down."

Clare winced at the memory. "Horrible things which weren't true," she said. "He was the man Marciano I told you about – the one who tricked me into going to the motel with him. Only he made it sound as if – if I had spent the night there with him and that I had deceived Bruno Cavour by doing so. You see, I hadn't told Oscar what you and Tarquin and the rest of you know about it. But he didn't stop to ask questions, he simply let fly. I was so dreadfully ashamed."

Eirene's eyes widened. "Why should you be? You didn't expect Oscar to sit there and *let* you be insulted?"

"At a private party where we were guests, he shouldn't have made a fisticuffs job of it, as Tarquin pointed out. It was so embarrassing for Jaquetta." Needing to know, Clare added, "What did Tarquin say about it after Oscar and I had left, do you know?"

"Nothing really to Nicola or me, except, on the way home, he said he hoped you hadn't had too cold a drive in Oscar's jalopy of a car. I asked him then why he had let you go, and he said it was by your own choice, he couldn't stop you. And perhaps it was just as well you did go," Eirene admitted, "considering the rather silly fuss Jaquetta made about it all."

"I suppose she had cause. It must have left a nasty taste, and I shall have to apologise to her."

"All the same, she needn't have taken it out on Tarquin, I thought."

"How do you know she did?"

"Eavesdropping."

"Oh, Eirene!"

"I couldn't help it. It was in the dance-room later. I was waiting for Frank to bring me an ice, and they were sitting on the far side of a huge potted palm. They didn't see me. They were speaking Italian, of course, and I didn't understand all that Jaquetta said, but I heard her ask Tarquin if he knew what the creature had said to you, and when he said he didn't know, she said 'Why not?' and *he* said, 'Because I didn't ask.' And then she went all upstage, saying she had only herself to blame – one should take better care as to whom one invited as one's guests. And I think she really turned on him when he reminded her – in what I call his ice voice – that as a member of his mother's household you, at least, were above reproach as a guest. She seemed quite put out at his daring to defend you, and she was still talking and spreading her hands when Frank came by with my ice and we moved off."

Clare sighed. "Oh dear. But what about you? Did you have a good party?"

"Super. Frank and I fit so well – dancing. And I met lots of other lovely men and at least Jaquetta was sweet with me, as she always is. I wish she liked you better than she seems to. I can't think why she doesn't," Eirene mused.

At breakfast Nicola greeted Clare as sunnily as usual and made no comment on the incident. But when they were alone

98

a little later she said, "I've had to tell Mama what happened last night. Anna had told her that you came home early, and of course she wanted to know why. I made as light of it as I could, but she said she would like to hear the details from you. So you'll tell her about it yourself, won't you?"

"Of course. Is she very annoyed?" asked Clare.

"Well, I think she wishes nothing like it had had to happen to upset Jaquetta's party. To Mama's generation good manners mean so much, and she may feel it reflects on Tarquin that you, as a kind of protegée of his, should have been the cause of a brawling match. But she is dressed and in her room, and if you go to her now you can be alone."

In her room the Signora was neither reading nor sewing. Erect and queenly as always, she sat, hands clasped in her lap, watching the door as if she had made a firm appointment with Clare, which it behoved the girl to keep. At sight of her, she lifted her spectacles and toyed with them. "Ah, child," she said. "Nicola will have asked you to come to me? Sit down, will you. You know why I wanted to see you, no doubt?"

Clare sat. "Yes, indeed," she agreed. "And I want to tell you how very sorry I am – "

Emilia Roscuro brushed the attempted apology aside. "There will be time enough for blame or no blame when I have heard what happened. So please tell me exactly what this man said and did to annoy you and to enrage your escort. In English, if you would find it easier," she added kindly.

"Thank you," Clare accepted. "Though do you want me to repeat all that he said?"

"Why not? I am a woman of the world. It cannot offend me, and I think I can guess what a virtuous girl would least like her escort to hear. Also what might rouse a chivalrous man to defend her – even to the point of violence. Well?"

Clare said again, "Thank you, *signora*," and told her who Florio Marciano was, and reported him verbatim.

99

"This was the man from whom you were escaping when Tarquin stopped to pick you up? And nothing of what he said was true?" the Signora questioned.

"Nothing."

"And the young man, Oscar Bridgeman, with whom you went to the Pallium, he is interested in you? Is fond of you?"

"He – says so."

"Declaring himself?" The Signora paused, as if considering her verdict. Then she conceded, "In that case one cannot expect him to behave in any other way than he did, and in my opinion he would have been more worthy of blame if he had not."

Infinitely grateful, Clare said, "I'm afraid Signorina Fiore was very much annoyed that two of her guests should have caused such a public spectacle at her party."

"Two? She blames you as the occasion of it?"

"She could be justified," Clare admitted.

"Nonsense, child. Jaquetta creates a volcano from a wisp of smoke, and she should be gratified that there are still men gallant enough to defend a woman's honour in the only way a bully understands – " The Signora broke off to call "Come in" to a knock on the door, and when Tarquin entered, she repeated herself for his benefit.

"You agree with me, son?" she demanded.

"It's for Jaquetta to agree with you or not, I think, Mama," he said.

"And I shall see that she does. But you, Tarquin – you know what scandal this wretch spoke of Clare, which caused her partner to knock him down?"

"Not in so many words. Only that Oscar Bridgeman considered she was insulted."

"Then I shall not ask Clare to repeat them a second time, but shall tell you myself," declared the Signora, and did so, concluding, "And so, such scurrility uttered in your hearing,

100

of a woman to whom you were attached – tell me, son, what would *you* have done?"

For a moment Tarquin's eyes met Clare's. Then he said, "I daresay, in Bridgeman's place, the same."

"Party or no party?" pressed his mother.

"Probably – party or no party," he agreed.

She frowned at that. "I do not like 'probably'. You are a man of spirit and a son of mine, and I should expect it of you. However, so far we are in accord, and Jaquetta must be asked to make no more of the unfortunate affair, you understand?"

Clare put in quickly, "Thank you, *signora*. But of course I shall apologise to her myself."

The Signora shook her head. "Not necessary at all," she ruled. "You say your partner apologised, and you were in no way to blame. So no more about it, please. You will be writing her a polite word of thanks for the party, of course, and perhaps some flowers would be a nice thought. But for the rest – let it drop, and I shall see, if Tarquin does not, that you hear no more about it. Yes, Tarquin? You have business to discuss with me?" she added, making her turn to him and her question a dismissal of Clare, who understood it as such and left them together, aware as she did so of the lift her spirits had known at Tarquin's guarded admission of "The same".

He and his mother had been at slight cross-purposes, of course – she, instancing any friend of his in need of his protection from slander; he, no doubt, envisaging Jaquetta put in the same false position as Clare had been. But in the moment when he had looked straight at her before answering the Signora's question, she could believe he had been thinking of her, though making the merest generality of his reply.

While the illusion lasted, she knew she was going to find it warming.

CHAPTER SIX

THE next thing to cause criticism and concern at the Casa was Eirene's acquisition of a motor-scooter. She was paying herself for its hire, it had the encouragement of Jaquetta, and in Eirene's view it bypassed successfully the Signora's edict against her riding pillion with Frank.

"Great-Aunt couldn't possibly mind my riding a bicycle – *if* one could, up and down these hills," she argued to Clare. "So what's the difference – a bicycle with an engine? And I gather the objection to my going pillion was that I'd have to hug Frank round his middle, on a machine of my own that bit of reasoning is out too."

"Not if the real difficulty was their not wanting you to be out with Frank alone. You know what different ideas they have from ours," Clare pointed out.

"Plugging sedately round the houses and into the country – in daylight?" Eirene scoffed. "You know I've never expected to go out after dark without you or Nicola or Jaquetta, and that, not half a dozen times since we've been here. Besides, Jaquetta thinks it's a good idea for me, and she has promised that she'll put in a word, or more than one, with Tarquin and with Aunt about it."

And so, at Jaquetta's silken persuasion that the scooter was no high-powered monster – in fact, no more than a useful toy, that Eirene was being stultified within the confines of the

Casa and the town, and that though Jaquetta was delighted to give much of her own time to "the child", there were occasions when she could not – Eirene was allowed to keep her scooter, with the proviso that she should always report where she was going on it, with whom, and how long she would be out.

To her credit, Eirene was meticulous about this, and though Clare knew that Nicola, for one, worried about her safety, she disarmed everyone by saying that she was no tyro; she had ridden a machine of the same make and low power in England, and it was "sheer bliss" to come and go as she pleased, as she had always done at home.

But as her new freedom made Clare's job more of a sinecure than ever, it became increasingly obvious, Clare thought, that Jaquetta was no disinterested party. Without a single overt move or open criticism of Clare, she had succeeded in driving a wedge between them. At first Clare had only suspected it; now she was pretty sure of it, though what was Jaquetta's purpose she had no idea.

That Jaquetta did not care for her, even Eirene knew. But on what score? Clare wondered. Snobbery perhaps? Eirene's close connection with the Roscuros was good enough for her; Clare, as Tarquin's "drowned little alien", was not. Could that be it? And if it were anything so petty, surely Jaquetta would derive more satisfaction from stressing her subordinate role as an employee, rather than encouraging her to a ladylike twiddling of her thumbs in idleness – which Clare felt she was often reduced to, for want of the job for which she had been engaged?

Unless – the thought had a cold insistence that there was something to it – unless that *was* the extreme of the purpose in Jaquetta's mind! That she had taken so deep a dislike to Clare as to want, and hope to be able to oust her from the Roscuro household by ultimately making it clear to Tarquin, to the Signora, to Nicola, to Eirene, that she wasn't needed there any longer. That she was a liability, no less.

Reluctant as she was to believe it, the suspicion rankled. Could that be Jaquetta's plan, and was it succeeding? The need of an answer sent Clare at last to Nicola, difficult though it was going to be to question Nicola without appearing to criticise Jaquetta, who was her friend.

It must be played lightly, Clare decided. She would make a joke of Eirene's independence of her company, watch for Nicola's reaction, but she would try to avoid mentioning Jaquetta by name.

Nicola, however, was none too helpful. In fact, she took Clare's careful broaching of the subject to mean that Clare wanted to leave.

"It's not that at all," Clare protested. "It's simply that I feel under-employed."

"Because Jaquetta entertains Eirene so much?" Nicola questioned.

"Because Eirene doesn't need a companion in quite the way you must have expected when you engaged me," Clare returned.

Nicola smiled wryly. "Well, of course we did not know then how much mistress of herself she would be. Sixteen only – young and shy, we thought. Needing someone to bridge the gap between her and us older folk. Nor could we foresee how kindly and generously Jaquetta would take to her – affording her so much of her own time to take her about and to see that she is neither lonely nor makes the wrong friends."

"But do you realise," urged Clare, "that since Signorina Fiore is so – kind, I feel I'm not necessary to Eirene in the same way?"

"Meaning that you would like to leave us? That you have some other post in view? Or even that – " Nicola stopped, then finished awkwardly, "Well, you did tell Mama that Signor Bridgeman had – spoken to you. So could it be that you are thinking of marriage?"

Clare searched her memory. What *had* she said to the Signora? Surely only that Oscar had said he liked her? After all, the rest that Oscar had admitted of his feeling for her was between themselves, and best forgotten for his sake. Yet here was Nicola jumping to the same conclusion that her mother must have done, turning Clare's innocent agreement that Oscar was attracted to her into an old-fashioned conviction that he must have "declared himself", "spoken" – in other words, had proposed!

She laughed, and saw Nicola's worried face clear. "Oscar Bridgeman certainly hasn't 'spoken' in the way I think you mean," she said. "In England we take rather longer to get to that stage than perhaps your people do. Oscar knows very little about me, or I about him, and if there were any question of an engagement between us, of course I'd have told you."

"And we should be very happy for you. Even though Tarquin – " Nicola broke off, flushing. "But perhaps I should not repeat to you what Tarquin has said of Signor Bridgeman," she finished.

"Shouldn't you? To me – as Oscar's friend?" Clare prompted gently.

"Well" – Nicola hesitated. "It was nothing bad or cruel, you understand? Just that Tarquin, as a business man himself, thinks him ill-advised to put all his capital into a property venture out here, knowing nothing of Italian business methods and with no great fluency in the language. But that is only Tarquin's opinion," she amended hastily. "You shouldn't repeat it to your friend, please."

"I certainly won't," Clare promised, though remembering that Tarquin's searching questions to Oscar on the night of the Pallium had implied just this – that he thought Oscar's plans rash in the extreme. Tarquin didn't mince his words in expressing a conviction, as she knew well. But that *was*

Tarquin Roscuro – part of the essence of a man she could respect as well as – love.

"And you won't speak any more of leaving us?" Nicola urged.

"Not if you think Eirene still needs me here."

"I think that all of us would be sorry to see you go – Mama, Tarquin, Eirene, the uncles – all. We grow used to you, grow fond of you. You are – of the family, as I hoped. Besides," Nicola smoothed the hips of her ripening figure, "I want you to see and admire my *bambino* when he arrives. My husband should be home for the event, and you must say whether you think the little one takes most after the Berninis or the Roscuros. I shall not mind which. They are both proud San Marino names."

Now the golden days of autumn had chilled and shortened. Though there were days when the sun still shone, on others the rain clouds piled angrily over the heights, deluged the town with their contents, dispersed and gathered again at the dictate of the tearing *garbino*, sweeping and eddying and lashing in turn, though usually itself dying down at sunset, leaving the night hours serene and calm.

Then, shortly before Christmas, starting at a very still dawn, San Marino's first snow of the winter fell. By the time the town was fully astir it was lying everywhere – a soft white pall on ground and streets as yet untrodden, a sparkling cake-icing on flat pantiled roofs, a bearing-down weight for trees and a conical hat for every domed turret and crenellation of the ancient walls.

But it was not going to last. In mid-morning the clouds which had brought it suddenly cleared, the sun came out in strength and there followed the telltale patter of thaw. Clare, wanting to use her camera on a transformation scene she had been told she might see only once in a San Marino winter, invited Eirene to go with her in search of some characteristic

106

shots of the town before the snow was gone. But Eirene begged off. She had other plans, now it had stopped snowing. She had telephoned to Frank; he was coming up and they were going to swim in Jaquetta's pool.

"One of those one-off happenings it'll be," she explained. "I've never yet gone swimming while there's been snow on the ground. I shall feel like one of those stouthearted bods who leap into the Serpentine or into the sea off Brighton beach on Christmas Day or whenever."

"Not that there's much of a parallel, considering the temperature to which the Fiores heat their pool," Clare commented.

She hadn't meant to sound sour, but supposed she must have done when Eirene took her up.

"You don't *mind* my going to swim?" Eirene asked anxiously.

"Of course not. Why should I?"

"Well, if you wanted me to go snapshotting with you. But I did ask Frank, and I don't care to put him off. He's probably started, anyway. So why don't you come along and swim too?"

"No, I'll get my pictures, I think, before the snow melts any further."

"O.K., if you'd really rather." It wasn't difficult to guess that Eirene was relieved that the swimming-party was to be a duet, not a trio.

But as it happened Clare was not to use her camera that day. Going to find Nicola to say she would be back to luncheon and to ask if Nicola needed anything from the town, she found Nicola on her knees in the *salotto*, engaged in a hilarious battle with one of the house kittens which had purloined a skein of Nicola's baby-wool from her workbasket and had succeeded in making of it not so much a cat's cradle as a kitten's prison house. His involvement with it, which must have begun as a game, was frightening him now, and the more frantically he

107

squealed and kicked to free himself, the closer he knitted the wool, cocoon-like, round his body.

Nicola, laughing and chiding him, "*Malvagio*!" was doing her best to free him with little result, and when Clare knelt beside her, she sat back on her heels, sucking a torn finger, and allowed Clare to take over.

"He could hardly have made a better job of it if he'd bought himself a knitting-pattern and begun by casting-on," quipped Clare as she lifted the squirming bundle on to her lap and began to lift loop after loop, one by one, from over his head and from round his flailing paws, only to find them caught again on some other part of his tubby person.

"My lovely angora wool! What is it going to be worth when he has done with it?" mourned Nicola.

"Or when it has done with him. I think it means to have its revenge. But never mind, I'll help you to wind it into a ball when they've both let go. It'll be safer that way," Clare promised, and did so when the wool was a limp tangle and the kitten, in the way of his kind, had collapsed on the hearth as if poleaxed and gone determinedly to sleep.

Nicola held the wool while Clare wound it, and Nicola had just let the last strand drift towards Clare for winding, when Tarquin came in. He looked at them both, then addressed Clare. "Where is Eirene?" he asked.

She told him. "Why, did you want her?" she added.

He shook his head. "No. You."

"Me?"

"If you are free. You weren't planning to join Eirene at Jaquetta's? No? I've a problem, and it occurred to me – " He broke off and turned to Nicola. "If you can spare her, I think Clare can help me out – at the kilns. Nurse Viere has gone sick, and as I'd rather not trouble the State Nurse to stand by at this time of year, if Clare would deputise for Viere in the clinic, I'd be grateful. What about it?"

Nicola said, "Oh, I think she would. Clare?"

"Of course, if you think I can help," Clare told Tarquin, who said, "It's just to have someone with nursing experience there if anything arises. But it's more likely that you'll find the job is a bit of a sinecure. Nobody may need your ministrations at all."

They were speaking English, and Nicola frowned over the word. " 'Sinecure' – what does that mean?" she asked.

Tarquin translated it, and she said, "Oh, but that is what Clare has complained of to me – that since Eirene spends so much time with Jaquetta, she finds she has too little to do herself."

"Really?" Tarquin looked at Clare. "What more, then, do you think you should be doing?"

"Well, more of the job you engaged me for – as a companion for Eirene," she admitted.

"Which you are still, aren't you?"

"Nominally, yes."

"And if you are here for Eirene when she needs you, and if we're content for her to find a second friend in Jaquetta, why complain? You haven't quarrelled with Eirene over this?"

"Oh, no. I haven't mentioned it to her."

"Then let's hear no more about it, until *we* decide you are superfluous, do you mind?" He turned back to Nicola. "I shall be lunching at the kilns, and so will Clare, in the clinic. I'll drive her back myself this evening, of course."

On the way over Clare asked what, broadly, her duties were and what she should do in the case of an emergency, should one occur.

"Much as you did with admirable efficiency that other time," Tarquin advised. "At the clinic you are on an outside telephone line, so if there's anything that calls for a doctor or an ambulance, you'll ring for them. In anything less urgent, I trust you to cope, though if you find yourself in difficulties, you can ring me on the internal line to my office. Anyway, you may find you have few patients or none, as I've said – it couldn't be, I hope, that you are actively jealous of Jaquetta Fiore in this matter of her friendship for Eirene?" he added in an abrupt switch of subject which took Clare aback.

Adjusting, she echoed, "Jealous? No. Why do you ask?"

"It had just occurred to me that you might imagine your nose – as your idiom has it – might have been put out of joint; feel, perhaps, that Jaquetta, Italian, rather beautiful and extremely sophisticated, has for Eirene the kind of mystique which you can't offer her. That could be, couldn't it?"

"Could be, perhaps. But it isn't," Clare said shortly.

He threw her a brief glance. "I'm sorry. And I suppose it's another thing again – the question of whether Eirene is in danger of being unduly flattered by Jaquetta's attention for her?"

Clare said, "That's not for me to judge. But if you are asking me, I'd say I don't think you need worry. Eirene is much too well-balanced and mistress of herself to have her head turned in that way."

Tarquin nodded. "You're probably right. She is the complete extrovert, though we couldn't have known how thoroughly she was going to fall on her feet before she arrived, could we?"

"No." On the verge of her impulse to ask him how much or how little he knew of Eirene's occasional traumatic despairs and resentments, she refrained. They were, after all, the girl's own secrets, their stress revealed only twice to Clare, who hadn't the right to discuss them with Tarquin, when, to all outward appearance, she wasn't troubled by them now.

Changing the subject, Clare asked idly, "You spoke of Signorina Fiore as Italian just now. Isn't she a Sammarinese, then?"

"Oh no, Italian by birth and upbringing. After her mother died her father wound up his business in Milan, set up again in

Rimini and chose to take a villa out here, rather than in the city. Which makes them," Tarquin added drily, "no more than acceptable aliens in the native view. Giorgio Fiore won't qualify for real citizenship in his lifetime, though Jaquetta will, if she marries one of us."

And you go afield for your women was a comment upon that which Clare, echoing his own words, thought but did not make aloud.

At the clinic her survey of its arrangements showed that Nurse Viere was admirably methodical. Every drawer and every shelf was labelled and carried a stock card of its present contents. There was a card index of patients' names and details, a locked drugs cupboard which contained nothing more lethal than some sedatives and pain-relievers, an adequate supply of bandages and splints and a number of common remedies which Clare had little trouble in identifying, for all their Italianized names. Evidently the clinic was more of a first aid post than a treatment centre, and as long as nobody turned up with too obscure an ailment, she was hopeful that her moderate skills and her very average Italian would be able to cope.

In fact, the morning produced only two emergencies – some stone-grit in an eye and the dressing on a blistered arm to be renewed. Tarquin had told her the time her luncheon would be served and she was expecting it when he himself came in.

"I thought we might lunch here together," he said. "I've ordered for you, do you mind? They do some very fair *tortellini* in the canteen. Parma ham to follow, and I thought you might prefer an ice to the cheese which I shall have."

The *tortellini*, which Clare had not had before, proved to be little twists of egg *pasta*, stuffed and under a rich sauce. The ham was served with braised celery and the ice was a *cassata*, full of diced fruit.

"If this is a sample of your regular menu, you do your employees well," she was commenting with a smile, when the telephone rang and she went to it.

She listened. "Who? Oh – " She looked across at Tarquin. "It's Oscar Bridgeman, wanting to speak to me. . . ."

"Where from? And how did he know where you were?"

"I don't know." She spoke and listened again, then said, "He came up to the Casa, hoping to find me, and Nicola told him he could ring me here. He has just finalised his contract for the land he has bought, and he wants me to lunch with him, by way of celebration."

"You've just had lunch," Tarquin pointed out.

"Yes."

"And the whole point of my enlisting your help being that I don't want the clinic unmanned until we close, I'd rather you didn't accept."

"But of course I won't." While Tarquin listened, she spoke again to Oscar, who offered, "Dinner tonight, then? Though I wanted to show you the site, and by then it will be too dark."

"Never mind. I can see it another time by daylight, and I'd like to dine. If that's all right?" she signalled to Tarquin, who nodded, rose and rang for the waitress to clear the meal. Of Oscar she asked, "Will you call for me, and when?"

"If you'll say what time you will be free, I'll come for you there."

"I shan't be dressed!"

"Doesn't matter. If I can't take you to the site, there's no point in carrying you down to Rimini. I'll stay up here and cool my heels at a movie, and then I know a cosy dive in the town where nobody does – dress, I mean. What time shall I collect you?"

She told him the hour the kilns closed and replaced the receiver. "He would like to come straight here for me," she told Tarquin.

"I see. Then you won't need me as chauffeur." He paused. "Is Nicola not to expect Eirene back to dinner either, then? If so, I'll tell her."

Clare frowned. "Oh, I don't know. Oscar didn't say. But I daresay he's inviting Eirene with Frank. I remember she claimed that at any celebration of his land deal, she and Frank must be there."

"But if not, it'll be dinner tête-à-tête for you and Bridgeman?"

"I shouldn't think so. With Eirene on the warpath, he wouldn't *dare*," Clare laughed, inviting a smile from Tarquin which she did not get. He merely said, "You'll be willing to come in again tomorrow, as I don't suppose Nurse Viere will be back? If so, I'll collect you, though rather earlier than I did this morning. Enjoy your evening."

Clare did. After Tarquin had left her, she had thought it good manners to ring Nicola herself to say that she would not be in to dinner, and then had settled to an afternoon which proved no more demanding than had the morning. She would have liked the chance to change into something more festive than a day-suit, but when Oscar had called for her, he was dressed equally informally in polo-neck and slacks, and had assured her she was 'perfect' for where he was taking her.

This proved to be a cellar restaurant close under the Cesta Tower – evidently the haunt of young Sammarinesi who had managed to slip the strict parental leash – its lighting only by candles in bottlenecks, its tables bare scrubbed wood, but its menu and service of five-star quality.

Since the night of Jaquetta's disastrous party Clare had already seen Oscar again. Once they had met for coffee with Frank and Eirene; once he had shown them his Rimini apartment, and both times his ease of manner towards her had been reassuring of his lack o resentment of her rejection of him. He had been kind then; he was kind still, making it easier for her to forget her guilt in having used him as a fantasy figure for Tarquin on that night. That madness was over now. She could put it behind her. It wouldn't happen again.

Tonight he hadn't invited Frank or Eirene to join them. "Time enough for the four of us to get together when we can lunch and go out to the site," he had said. "Besides, they had better make hay in each other's company while the sun shines. For once we get to work, Frank will be nose-down to the job I brought him out to do."

He had ordered champagne and had been eager with plans and hopes during the meal. Afterwards they dawdled at leisure over their coffee and liqueurs, watched other couples dancing, but did not join them on the pocket-handkerchief square of floor space. Though they had dined early it was nearly midnight when they left and drove back to the Casa.

Throughout the evening Oscar had made no intimate move towards Clare, and when he got out of the car with her he still made none. They had been two friends enjoying each other's company, no more, and she was grateful to him. But when he took her hand as she was above him by the height of the broad portico's step, a little light of head and her mood easy, she had a crazy impulse to reward him – and bent, uninvited, to brush his lips with her own.

She straightened, smiling, hearing his half caught breath of surprise and pleasure at the same moment as she was aware that the shaft of light in which they both stood was due to the door behind her having opened for the emergence of the figure who now stood just off from her shoulder – Tarquin.

He said coolly, "I'm sorry. Shall I leave the door open for you? Are you just going in?"

"Yes, at once."

"Goodnight, then." With a gesture in Oscar's direction he walked out into the square, and the darkness swallowed him.

Clare said shakily, "That was – silly."

Oscar grinned. "Silly, you say? Do it again, any time, anywhere, and you'll find me willing!"

"I only meant it to say goodnight and thank you for a lovely, lovely evening."

His grin faded. "You weren't feeling sorry for me? Throwing me a crust?"

"Of course not!"

"Then I'm going to take the liberty of returning it in kind – "

But his kiss, though firmer than hers for him, was only brief before, turning her about, he urged her towards the open door of the house, and she was alone with her image of Tarquin's witness of a kiss which she had meant to be as guileless and playfully offered as a child's, though to an onlooker it could well have looked like invitation. She wished they were on the kind of terms which would enable her to laugh it off if he teased her about it. But she knew he would not. Though he appeared to accept her friendship with Oscar, he seemed to have reserves about it which he had never voiced.

Two days later Nurse Viere returned to duty and then Christmas was only a week away. The streets of the town became a toy fair of booths selling everything from dolls to tricycles, from boardgames to printing sets. There were sweetmeat stalls of nougat and sticks of toffee straight from the boiling, and animal shapes of almond paste and of course San Marino's own sweet cake, the *cacciatello*.

On every street were stalls of figurines – of San Marino soldiery and of the Christ Child and of the angels and the Kings, and the mild animals which would gather about the Manger in the Christmas Crib which, fashioned from sheets of cork-bark, would appear in every home. On the main square a shrouded Nativity scene was being built for unveiling on Christmas Eve before the torchlight procession to

Midnight Mass in the Basilica, when all San Marino would be there.

Father Christmas, in the shape of Saint Nicholas, was to be seen around in person, but his rival, the witch Befana, being airborne by broomstick, was not. Clare and Eirene learned that she merely brooded invisibly over the Christmas and the Twelfth Night scenes and whereas Father Christmas made his gifts wholly benevolently, Befana, who showered presents too, tied conditions to hers – all the good children being rewarded with goodies in their stockings, the bad ones with lumps of coal. Befana also ran a system of mischievous forfeits, as Clare was to learn from – of all the least likely people to be hand-in-glove with wizardry – Tarquin . . .

Christmas at the Casa was a simple, homely occasion, linked more closely to the mystery of the Nativity than were the adult Christmas festivities in England, Clare thought. Nicola, lovingly building the Crib all week and dressing the tree; Tarquin, installing and testing fairy lights; the uncles acknowledging the twentieth century for once by going shopping for presents; the Signora appointing an undisturbed afternoon in her room for the wrapping of hers; Eirene and herself going shopping separately and being as furtive as everyone else with secret hoards of parcels.

Clare supposed it was so in every real family. In fact she remembered it had been so for her too while she had one. But of latter years her Christmases had been spent either on the wards in hospital or in being invited to sit in at friends' gatherings for the day. It was something new for her to be drawn into this family circle as if she were part of it.

She bought simple, modest presents for the Roscuros – among them, flowers for the Signora, initialled handkerchiefs for the uncles, a fine mohair stole for Nicola, a driving-mirror for Eirene's scooter, a small watercolour of a picturesque corner of the town for Tarquin. Eirene's choice was mostly fun gifts, with everyone remembered, down to the house cat and her kittens.

It seemed there was a tradition, by edict of the Signora, that only presents to and from the immediate family and the staff were hung on the Christmas tree. No outsiders were invited to the meals of Christmas Day, but Anna and her scullery-maid and the odd-job boy came, as of right, to the present-opening and mid-morning wine and sweetmeats. When Tarquin had distributed all the parcels, everyone took it in turn to open one of theirs for showing round to all the rest and for lavishing thanks upon the giver.

It was a sharing of pleasure and gratitude which Clare enjoyed very much, and, strictly true or not, the phrases, "Just what I wanted" and "How did you guess I should like that?" had as heartwarming a ring in Italian as in English.

At the final round it was her first turn to open, with everyone else having one more parcel to go. She knew the giver of this one and she had saved it until last. Opening it, she hoped it was not something too ephemeral, like perfume or chocolates, but something she could keep to remind her of Tarquin and of the one Christmas when she had shared his home.

The wrappings were off now and she gasped with surprise and pleasure. They were all looking at her, she knew, as her hands curved about the swelling body of the vase he had allowed her to handle on her first visit to the kilns, the acanthus-decorated piece which he had said was unique, its design never to be repeated. And he had given it to her! It had no twin; no one would ever buy one like it "from stock", he had told her. Yet, at whatever quixotic impulse of generosity, he had given it to *her*.

As the others admired it and Eirene wanted to hold it, she looked across at him wordlessly, wondering how to thank him. Neither "Just what I wanted" or "How did you guess –?" would do. For she had never dreamed of possessing it, and he hadn't guessed – he had remembered, which was better. At last she managed, "I can't think of anything at all that would please me more," and was warmed by his smile and his genuine, "I'm glad".

When the others had opened their last parcels Tarquin poured wine for everybody and they all wished each other a seasonal *felice Natale.* Then they dispersed, carrying off their assorted bundles of presents and before returning to the kitchen Anna clucked, "Tch! Tch!" over the litter of Christmas paper and tissue and gay tags and strings in which the carpet of the *salotto* was nearly ankle-deep. She sent back a maid, armed with a big cardboard carton, to collect it, but Clare, who hadn't yet left the room, offered, "Leave the carton, and I'll see to it," as Tarquin came back after carrying his mother's presents to her room for her.

He stayed to help. So had the kittens, darting and plunging and rolling, and killing every trailing string with deadly intent. They clawed up the sides of the carton and hid in it; tunnelled under wrapping paper and tore tissue to shreds with sharp little teeth.

Tarquin, recovering a wriggling tabby from the carton for the nth time, commented, "The cleaning of the Augean stables would have had nothing on this as an impossible task," and Clare, patiently rewinding a rough ball of twine, laughed and agreed.

They gradually effected a clearance and the kittens, baulked of their prey, ambled off to pastures new. Tarquin returned to the drinks tray, poured for himself and pointed to a half-full wineglass which Clare remembered having set down.

"Someone didn't finish theirs," he said.

"No. It's mine. I forgot it." She went over to get it.

"Do you still want it?"

"Yes, please."

They stood side by side and drank. As Tarquin put down

118

his empty glass, Clare did the same and was about to take up her pile of parcels when he asked, "Do you know yourself the scene of the picture which you gave me?"

"Oh yes," she said. "That was why I chose it – because when I came upon that corner of the Via Belucci one day, I thought someone ought to paint it, and then I found someone had."

"No ambitions of your own that way?"

She shook her head. "I'm no artist, I'm afraid."

"Another of the skills you claim not to have?"

"One of the many. And artistically I can only look and enjoy. I can't do or make."

"And you are going to enjoy your vase?"

"Oh *yes*, it's lovely. And I'm so grateful that you remembered how I admired it. The only one of its design too!"

Tarquin laughed. "It's not the Koh-i-Noor, nor even the Portland Vase. And it's only this season's 'unique'. Next year we shall design another." He paused. "It's breakable, you know."

"Of course. But I pray I shan't break it."

He slanted a glance at her. "You don't get the drift?"

She frowned, puzzled. "Drift?"

"No one has told you about the forfeit that our national witch, Befana, demands shall be paid in exchange for a breakable gift?"

"No. You mean – " she searched for a parallel – "something in the way that, when we give a present of a knife or a pair of scissors, we give a coin too, so that they shan't cut love between the giver and the taker?"

"Something like that. Except" – there was a dark mischief in his eyes which she had never seen there before – "except that Befana lays down the precise nature of the forfeit to be exacted, on pain of the gift's spontaneously cracking before midnight, if the forfeit isn't exchanged – "

"And what is the forfeit she wants?"

"*She* doesn't want it. She only rules that it be exchanged. And it's – this."

With a hand about her wrist he had turned her to face him, and her one thought before he kissed her was that this time it needn't be phantasy; it ought to be true.

For these weren't Oscar's arms holding her; they were Tarquin's, and these were his lips, close now, about to take hers, demanding her surrender of them as his right. She should be willing and eager to yield to the ecstasy of a moment she had thought would never be hers to enjoy. She ought to be ready to respond, to give, to melt, and to such a first kiss there should be an afterwards of shared delight in the essential rightness of it; in the sureness that it would happen again – and again – for love.

Yet it wouldn't. For it wasn't true. It was all false. This was Tarquin, making unfair male opportunity, and this was Clare, about to be betrayed into the pretence that the taking and the giving would be real and meant. And they wouldn't be –

But as if he didn't appreciate the distinction between kissing a girl for love and kissing her as a sop to a piece of silly folklore, he made the pressure of his mouth upon hers long and hard and searching, while she forced herself to tense against him, a prisoner waiting for release.

And when it was over the same instinct for self-defence kept her comment light. "You've evidently had long training under the mistletoe," she said. "Or in the giving of fragile presents."

"And you not enough," he retorted. "No grace. No verve."

That hurt, but it told her what she wanted to know – that she had shown him nothing of her hunger, her need. Lightly still, "And does Befana insist on – verve?" she asked.

"I'd say she expects a forfeit to be at last an exchange – not the one-sided trespass that was."

"And you think she won't be satisfied with it?" Clare gathered her parcels again. One slipped from her grasp. He stooped to retrieve it, replaced it carefully on the top of the pile.

"That remains to be seen," he said. "You'll have to 'ware midnight, won't you?"

CHAPTER SEVEN

CLARE half expected her pleasure in the acanthus vase to be spoiled by the incident. But it wasn't. She stood the vase on the window-ledge of her room where, at that height, its only background was the sky, and where its graceful lines were a delight which greeted her every morning on waking.

In the market she bought button-blossomed sprays of mimosa for it, and it was when she was crossing the hall carrying a bunch of this that Tarquin, meeting her, made his first and only reference to the piece of fiction he had offered her on Christmas morning. Seeing she was about to go up the stairs and evidently drawing his conclusions from the flowers she held, he asked, "You find it still holds water, then?"

Clare halted, one foot on the bottom stair. "The vase? Of course. As I always knew it would."

His eyes smiled. "Such Anglo-Saxon phlegm! Can you swear, hand on heart, that you didn't lie awake until midnight, waiting for it to crack?"

"None of us went to bed before midnight on Christmas night, as you know. You were still here yourself," she reminded him."

"Ah yes," he nodded. "And so Befana didn't do her worst after all?"

Going along with the absurdity of all this, "Did you really expect that she might?" Clare asked gravely.

"It was possible, I thought. But either it was one of her off-days for casting spells, or she appreciated that I had done *my* best, or, of her charity, she gave you the benefit of the doubt as to whether you may have done yours. I could have told her differently – that you weren't really trying. But you can count on being safe now. It can't and won't happen now."

"You mean my vase is safe?"

"You and your vase. If only because, as the saying goes, Christmas comes but once a year – "

And you won't try to kiss me again, and I shan't be here next Christmas, thought Clare bleakly as she went on up the stairs. And then – just how superstitious could the Latins get? – only to be glad, in the very moment of asking herself the question, that Tarquin *was* Latin enough to *be* superstitious. For, as once before, when he had revealed that he could be jealous of his rights, it showed there were other disarming and lovable chinks in his armour of efficiency and family pride and the authority which no one but his mother ever questioned. It showed he was human and, however hopelessly, Clare loved him for it.

It was to be very shortly after Christmas, and before Oscar and Frank returned from a skiing trip in the Italian Alps, that it occurred to her how little Eirene seemed to be seeing of Jaquetta these days. For some time Clare refrained from comment. But when Eirene, casually questioned as to her plans for the day, never now seemed to be going down to the villa to swim or out anywhere in Jaquetta's company, Clare realised there must have been some rift between them, though she thought it wise to wait for Eirene to tell her its cause.

Meanwhile Eirene either roamed the house, looking bored, or joined Nicola or Clare whenever they were going out, or went out and returned alone on her scooter, and always contrived to disappear whenever Jaquetta came up to the Casa, as was her habit, to see Nicola.

And so it was Jaquetta herself who was to enlighten Clare. She arrived one afternoon when Nicola was resting and Clare was alone in the *salotto*, waiting for Eirene to join her for a game of Scrabble. Anna showed Jaquetta in. Eirene, evidently primed by having seen Jaquetta's car outside, did not appear. A few minutes later they both heard the sputter of Eirene's scooter engine; Clare, putting away the Scrabble letters and the board, said unnecessarily, "Eirene seems to have decided to go out," and Jaquetta, with the thin smile she kept for non-amused occasions, said, "And naturally we both know why, don't we? The poor child is shy of facing me!"

Clare agreed, "Yes, I think she has been avoiding meeting you lately. But – shy of you? Why should she be? What has she done to make her so?"

Jaquetta spread an expressive hand. "My dear, should you have to ask me that?" she queried. "You must know that it is nothing she has done, but what you have done yourself to spoil our friendship, to come between her and the amusement and the help I think I was able to give her, and which you couldn't, to at all the same degree. A friendship, however, which I had *no* intention should be questioned and undermined by petty jealousies like yours, and therefore it had to end. So end it I did – rather cruelly, I'm afraid. The child took it quite badly."

Clare knew that she must have whitened with anger. "You told Eirene that you didn't want to see her any more, or take her about or invite her to your house, because you had dared to conclude – without a word to or from me – that I was jealous of the attention you've given her; that I was jealous of *you*?"

Jaquetta shook her head. "Oh no, I spared you that. I'm no trouble-maker for the sake of it. No, I merely told *her* that from now on I was going to find myself too occupied to entertain her, and that as I couldn't always be tied to playing chaperon to her, I'd rather she didn't come to the villa unless I invited her, and not to arrange to meet her young playfellow there. But *you* I expected to know exactly why I had to issue this fiat, and I find it difficult to believe that you don't."

Clare said icily, "I think you must try, *signorina*. I tell you I didn't know why you had suddenly abandoned your interest in Eirene. I do now, because you've told me. But there's not a grain of truth to your conclusions, and I'm going to say again that you had no right to jump to them – without any evidence of my reactions at all."

"You think not?" Jaquetta's tone was silky. "Not even on your *own* evidence, on the things you have said yourself?"

"Such as?" Clare invited.

"But surely! Why, the complaints you have chosen to carry to Nicola and to Tarquin about my very sincere interest in Eirene. Claiming, I understand, that I had ousted you; that you had had your own charge of the child usurped by me; that you resented taking second place to me, and that you – "

Clare cut in there. "You are saying that Nicola has reported all this to you?"

"Not Nicola. She has accepted my excuse that I have too too many commitments to trouble further with Eirene, and she is grateful for all the time I have given to the child up till now. No, I should have known nothing of your petty grudge against me if Tarquin hadn't chosen to dare to take *me* to task for monopolising Eirene to the exclusion of you! I was incensed, and I let him know it."

"Though you shouldn't forget, should you," Clare advised, "that it was you who suggested to me that I might well find myself without a job if Eirene continued to prefer your company to mine, and to find more profit in it?"

Jaquetta shrugged. "A joke, that was all."

"Was it? To me it sounded like a serious warning that if they found me superfluous, the Roscuros wouldn't hesitate to get rid of me."

"I only hinted that Tarquin mightn't think twice about it. Nicola is too kind-hearted. And I wasn't to know that you would run to both Nicola and Tarquin with complaints against me," Jaquetta claimed.

"I spoke to Nicola, yes," Clare admitted. "But not in complaint against you. I simply said that I felt I wasn't making myself fully useful, and that perhaps Eirene didn't need me as much as they had originally expected."

"If you were sincere about that, I'd have thought you would offer to leave," suggested Jaquetta sourly.

"Which Nicola claimed to fear, but said they wouldn't hear of it. And I didn't 'run to' her brother at all. It was he who brought up the subject with me and left me in no doubt whatsoever that they expected and wanted me to stay."

"Leaving me as the pawn who takes the blame for doing no more than she saw as a charity to a raw teenager, handed over to the care of another teenager, little older or more polished than herself!" raged Jaquetta. "I've taken Eirene about, introduced her to my friends, spent money on her, given her presents, covered up for her when she – I suppose she has never let you guess just *how* often she has been out with that callow English boy alone?"

Clare stared, aghast. Up till now her clear conscience had kept her in command of the situation, but now she was not. She had to *ask* something of Jaquetta; ask, fearing the answer lest it had to be true. She said, "Are you implying that Eirene has let you shield her when she has wanted to do something which she promised the Roscuros faithfully that she wouldn't do?"

Jaquetta shrugged again. "What else? She is raw, as I have said. And wild. English, and expecting to be allowed to run about as she pleases and with whom. Anyway, I'm not her keeper. *You* are," she finished rudely.

"But her people trusted her with you. And you needn't have encouraged her in deceiving them by asking Frank Bridgeman to your party, need you? As it were, approving him for her?"

"She would have sulked if I hadn't."

"Eirene *never* sulks!" Clare defended her.

"Which, right or wrong, I've no intention of proving from now on. I am finished with her. She is your charge now and I wish you joy of your task. Though I warn you – and this time I'm *not* joking," Jaquetta added – "that once you fail Tarquin Roscuro in the smallest degree, you will get short shrift from him, very short indeed."

"So you said before, and I don't think you were joking that time either." Clare paused. And then, her mingled chagrin and anger unable to resist the gibe, "Speaking from experience perhaps, were you?" she insinuated, and saw the banked fury in the other girl's eyes as Nicola came into the room, all welcoming smiles.

For her part, Clare couldn't wait to clear her decks of the doubts of Eirene's good faith which Jaquetta had put into her mind. She had no opportunity to be alone with the other girl until they went to bed, but then she went to Eirene's room with her questions ready.

"I thought we were going to play Scrabble this afternoon. But you went out instead. Why?" she asked.

Eirene fingered a lock of her hair into a grotesque twist. "You must know why," she told the mirror she was facing, her back to Clare. "I'd seen Jaquetta's car outside, of course."

"And you didn't want to see her?"

"She wouldn't have wanted to see me."

"I don't think she did." Clare was candid. "But I'd have liked to know you were handy, so that you could say whether or not some accusations she made against you were true."

Eirene twisted another hank of hair. "Accusations? What kind of? What about?" she asked, her tone listless.

"Well, for instance, have you ever told me or Nicola or anyone here that you were going down to Jaquetta's villa and would be with her, when in fact you were going out alone with Frank?"

The effect of that was electric. Eirene spun round on the dressing-stool, listless no longer, but wide-eyed with indignation. "But *of course* I've been out with Frank on our scooters! You know I have, and I've *always* told them –!"

Clare said, "That's not the point. What I asked was – Have you ever pretended you were with Jaquetta when you weren't at all?"

"*Never*! Never once. I *promised* them I would always say where I was – truthfully where I was – and I always have. You believe me, don't you? Clare, you must!"

It was impossible not to trust such vehemence. "Of course I do, and I'm terribly glad," Clare said.

"But *she* told you differently? Said I had sheltered behind her, that I had lied to all of you?"

Clare nodded. "I couldn't bear to believe it, so I had to ask you."

"But there wasn't any need for me to lie. They've always let me go to meet Frank whenever I've said." Eirene turned away again. Elbows on the dressing-table, fists against each cheek, she muttered, "How could she? How *could* she? I thought she liked me. She said she enjoyed taking me about, and when I asked her why she went to so much trouble for me, she told me not to be silly. And then suddenly she was 'too busy', she said. And now this – She even lies about me!" A fist came down with a thump. "Well, I won't take it! To-morrow I shall go straight down to the villa and ask her to explain herself, make her tell me why!"

But there Clare was adamant. "You'll do nothing of the

sort," she said. "You couldn't win, and you are not, repeat *not*, to make trouble between Jaquetta and your people over something she won't dare to say to anyone else, knowing it isn't true."

"She said it to you."

"Because, I think, she wanted to hurt me through you, hoping I would believe you had been too clever for me. She has never liked me, as I think you know," Clare added.

"But –"

"Leave it." Clare stood up. "Forget it. You know you aren't guilty and so do I, and I'm probably the only person to hear it from her."

"But if she did say it to anyone else, you'd stand up for me?"

Clare smiled. "What do you think?"

"All right. If you say so," Eirene allowed reluctantly as she began to undress. A few minutes later, in shortie nightgown and barefoot, she looked round Clare's door.

"Play you at Scrabble tomorrow, if you like," she offered.

"O.K. English or Italian words?"

"I don't mind. You choose."

"We'll toss for it," said Clare. "Goodnight." As the door closed she silently thanked Eirene's volatile nature which could seemingly throw off trouble like a discarded garment. But she was to learn she had been grateful too soon. She thought she had not been asleep more than half an hour when she woke to the – unmistakable this time – sound of Eirene's sobbing, and this time Clare did not hesitate. Without stopping for either robe or slippers, she went across to the other room, stood beside Eirene's prone figure, covered only by a sheet, and laid a hand upon her shoulder.

Eirene shook it off. "Go away."

"No." Clare sat beside her on the bed. "Tell me? What's the matter?"

"Go away." Eirene's voice was muffled in the pillow. "I hate you all!" A pause. "Oh no, not you. But the rest of them, the lot."

"You don't hate them. Not Nicola – that's impossible. Nor Tarquin. And not your great-aunt Emilia – she's a bit regal, but she is kind. Nor the uncles – how could you? Besides, they are your own people, your family!"

If it had occurred to Clare she might have wondered that she, who only a few months earlier had scorned "family" as an empty, spurious, betraying concept, should now be pleading its virtues as if she knew their value. But Eirene erupted angrily to the word.

"Family!" she scorned, sitting up. "That's what I hate. Not them, one by one. But they're so – *cosy* inside it, so beastly sure that it's got all the answers –"

"Perhaps, for them, it has. And you belong to it yourself," Clare reminded her.

"Not me!"

"You can't help yourself."

"I can. I'm English. It's all very well for them. According to Uncle Paolo, generations of them have married and lived happily ever after, a lot of them here in this – this fortress, until they died and their eldest son took over. And it's just the same pattern for this lot. There are the uncles, contented cabbages both of them, and Nicola, happily married and expecting a baby, and Tarquin's mama, who'll turn into a gracious dowager when he marries Jaquetta –"

Clare felt her heart plunge. " 'When'? Do you know he's going to?"

"*She* says so. And so it will start all over again, and no wonder they can be so smug about the family, with everything going for them. They just don't know what it is not to be one or have one. Look at us – a father Landor and a mother Landor, and a daughter Landor – me. And though we used to belong, we don't any more. We – we're just three separate people, and it's all – all *horrible*. But that's something they wouldn't understand." And with a savage thump at her pillow Eirene flung herself face downwards again.

Clare said, "I'm sure they would try, if you would let them; if they knew how much you care. Besides, they must have understood the situation enough when they invited you here to allow your parents to be apart for a while and to get their bearings. I think I'd hand it to the Roscuros to know that you shouldn't have been left to oné of them, sort of weighting the balance, as it were. And I don't think you should take it out on the Roscuros, because they've done their best to make you happy here, and you have been, mostly, haven't you?"

"Thanks to Frank and my scooter – and having you."

"And you wouldn't have had any of us if they were really as stuffy as you make them out to be." Clare hesitated over a delicate question. "Don't answer if you'd rather not," she said, "but do you know what it is between your mother and father? There – isn't anyone else for either of them?"

"Oh no." Eirene sat up and began to pick at the sheet. "They married for love, and for Mummy no other man exists but Daddy – still. And *he's* never had time to look at another woman, because that's the trouble, you see. His work – he lives for it; eats and drinks and sleeps it, and has to travel a lot, and we hardly ever see him. And it got to the point where I think Mummy couldn't stand it any more, and though English Grandma – that's Daddy's mother – says they should have their heads banged together, they decided to have at least six months apart and see what happened."

"And is anything? Happening, I mean?" asked Clare.

"I don't know. I've told you – they never mention each other when they write to me." Calmer now, Eirene seemed to notice when Clare give a little shiver. "You didn't put on your dressing-gown and you've nothing on your feet," she accused.

"You're not so adequately covered yourself," smiled Clare.

"I'm all right now." Eirene snuggled under the sheet and pulled up a light blanket. "It was just that – that Fiore woman turning me down, and – and everything. I'll get over it. But Clare –" as the latter reached the door – "aren't you as glad as I am that neither of us will be here when she's queening it here as Tarquin's wife?"

And when Uncle Paolo, in his beautiful script, writes her name linked to Tarquin's in the family chart, thought Clare. Aloud she said to Eirene's question, "Yes, I suppose we shall both be back in England then." And wished with all her heart that it hadn't to be so. For then, unlike Eirene, she would not be even one of three separate people. She would be one, alone.

Tarquin had given no sign of his having noticed Jaquetta's desertion of Eirene, and Nicola had accepted Jaquetta's excuse that she was going to be too busy to play escort over the next few weeks. Eirene continued to roam discontentedly while Frank and Oscar were still away, and when they were due back Clare was thankful to be able to dangle the small carrot of Oscar's promise that the four of them would go to view his building site and enjoy a celebration luncheon.

But though Frank rang Eirene to say he was back, he proffered her only a vague "See you soon" invitation to meet, and Clare heard nothing at all from Oscar. Eirene grumbled, "That's just like men. They pick you up and then drop you as they would a hot potato." To which cynical axiom Clare teased in reply, "And with all your experience at sixteen, of course you'd know, wouldn't you?" But she had to admit she was a little puzzled herself at Oscar's silence, until the morning when he did ring to say that he "had" to see her.

"I can't come up for you, because my car is in dock and I have to wait in to see a man – my solicitor – urgently. But do you think you could manage to come down?"

Clare looked at her watch and calculated. "Yes, I could

catch the bus, but I'm afraid Eirene is out."

"Doesn't matter. It's you I want to see. If you can get down within the next hour, I should be free by then."

"All right. Where shall I meet you?"

"Better call for me here, and I'll take you to lunch while we talk."

"Then I must ask Nicola if she minds my being out for lunch here." Clare paused. "What is it, Oscar? What's the urgency? You sound worried."

"And you can say that again," he agreed emphatically. "But I won't talk now. I'll explain when I see you."

His apartment was above a shop on a busy street. It and its twin across a corridor were reached from a door on to the street and a flight of stairs, and when Clare arrived, he was just seeing his solicitor out.

"Bless you for getting here," he said. "Let's go." His hand beneath her elbow led her down again to the street, where he hailed a taxi and gave the driver directions to a restaurant on the esplanade. There, when they had ordered, Clare asked again, "Tell me now what's happened. For something has, hasn't it?"

He nodded, his mouth grim. "I've been conned," he said.

"*Conned*? What do you mean? Not over –?"

He nodded again. "That's right. Over the land I've bought and paid for – more fool me."

"But you've bought it and paid for it," Clare echoed foolishly. "It's already yours!"

"And about as much value as a building site for luxury villas as if it were so many hectares of potato patch. And why? You may well ask. Because, within a year or less, a good commercial auto-route is going to run straight through it, that's why. And even if the fringes were left to private ownership, who, you tell me, is going to choose a retiring home or a cosy love-nest, cheek by jowl to a motorway?" Oscar retorted savagely.

"But you should have been told before you bought. *Someone* must surely have known?" Clare protested, aghast.

"And I haven't much doubt that somebody did – the previous owners, the vendors."

"And who –? Oh!" Clare had remembered. "That was Giorgio Fiore, Jaquetta Fiore's father – his firm!"

"Who recognised a mug when they saw one, and decided to clean him out. It was as simple as that."

Clare persisted, "But other people must have known too. The plans for the new road must have been available somewhere, and shouldn't your solicitor have known they existed?"

"He swears he didn't, and I don't know whether to believe him or not. For all I'm aware, he may have been in it with Fiore and is due to take his cut. No, all he does is to claim baby-innocence, wring his hands and quote *caveat emptor* at me."

"What does he mean by that?"

"Latin for 'Let the buyer beware' – in other words, look well before you leap into a purchase, for you'll get neither sympathy nor redress afterwards, when you've parted with your cash. It's not only a quaint old Italian custom, though. I've known people to be caught by it all my estate agency life. And then I ignore the possibility myself! But I *wanted* that land, Clare, and I didn't investigate as I should have done." Oscar paused. "Or perhaps I'm being unfair to myself there. I did try at first to root for snags, but always they blocked me and dangled the threat of someone else jumping in and buying it over my head."

"*Who* blocked you?"

"Fiore, the smooth-tongued so-and-so – through my man, who seemed often to be more on his side than on mine. You know, Clare, I ought to have listened to Tarquin Roscuro when he warned me I might fall in with sharks. But how was I to know they were sharks? And he stopped short of telling me so."

Clare was shocked at the implication of that. "But Tarquin couldn't know that Signor Fiore was tricking you. He *couldn't* suspect Fiore was capable of sharp practice, or he would have gone further and warned you," she maintained loyally.

"With no possible interest in my welfare, and he more or less engaged to the man's daughter?" Oscar doubted. "Meanwhile, I'm left holding the baby, and what do I do now? Sell it to the next tenderfoot who happens along?"

"You couldn't do that. It wouldn't be honest."

He sighed. "That was supposed to be a joke – ha, ha. As if there *were* any potential buyers as gullible as I've been. What a hope! Even if I could sell it now, it would be at a dead loss."

Over the meal which neither of them enjoyed, they argued the problem back and forth, unable to leave it alone. At one point Oscar said intensely, "You know *why* I wanted the scheme to succeed, don't you? Because I meant it should prove myself to you; that I had to show you I wasn't the fool in business which Roscuro seemed to think me?"

Clare said, "You didn't have to succeed in anything to keep me as your friend. You must know that."

"At first I didn't. You were so surrounded by wealth and success – the Roscuros', the Fiores', their friends' –"

"But not part of it. I don't belong."

"All the same, I thought you must be impressed, if not a little bewitched by it. And by the time I realised you weren't, I wanted you for more than a friend. I hoped that by the time Eirene went home I'd have the project well enough in hand to allow me to ask you to marry me a bit later."

Clare said unhappily, "I've told you, I'd always want you for a friend, whether you were successful or not."

"But that doesn't stop me from hoping for more, and I shall still, until you give me a definite No."

She knew she ought to tell him he had had her definite No. But she hadn't the courage to add to this present troubles. She only knew she must never encourage him again as she had done with that kiss which Tarquin had witnessed and which she still blushed to remember.

It was not until he had seen her to her return bus, kissing her cheek lightly at parting, that her own plan began to form in her mind.

It was Tarquin who had warned Oscar against doing business in a language and conditions which he didn't fully understand. So who better than Tarquin to suggest a solution – always supposing there were one which wouldn't leave Oscar ruined?

But in going to Tarquin she knew she must lay the blame on Oscar's failure to investigate before parting with his money. It was, after all, only Oscar's strong suspicion that he had been wilfully deceived, and in view of the Roscuros' links with the Fiores', she mustn't accuse Jaquetta's father to Tarquin without proof.

She didn't know how she might contact him alone. But that night she was in luck. Signora Roscuro had a headache and had had a supper tray taken to her room. Nicola, who had lately gained Eirene's lacklustre interest in making a dress for herself, took Eirene to the breakfast-room to cut it out. Lucio Marini was giving a lecture in the Cesta Armoury on the military relics of Garibaldi, and before dinner Tarquin had driven him and his brother there, afterwards returning to the Casa. Which, when Nicola and Eirene departed after they had drunk their coffee, left Tarquin and Clare together.

Nicola had relinquished the coffee tray to Clare. Tarquin wanted a second cup, which he took from her, asked her permission to light a cigar and stood with his back to the deep hearth where a fire of logs burned.

Clare stiffened her resolve over several sips from her own

cup. Then she said as introduction, "Oscar Bridgeman invited me down to Rimini to have lunch with him today."

Tarquin inclined his head. "So I heard. He entertained you at his apartment, didn't he?"

Clare stared, puzzled. Nicola could have mentioned that she had gone to meet Oscar, but Nicola couldn't know something that wasn't true.

"Oh no," she said. "He took me to Tre Penne on the front."

"Then Jaquetta must have been wrong in saying that when she was shopping in the Via Rivetta she saw you leaving the building where Eirene had told her Bridgeman and his nephew live."

"Implying that I had lunched there with Oscar? I'd only called for him, as he'd had to see his solicitor!" Was she never to be free of Jaquetta's pinpricks of malice? Clare wondered.

"Implying nothing," said Tarquin. "Simply mentioning that she had seen you. Did you like Tre Penne? It has a good reputation."

"Yes. I hadn't been there before. But I'm afraid we weren't in the mood to appreciate the food, as Oscar has come up against some bad trouble, and he wanted to tell me about it."

"Trouble? How bad?"

"About as bad as it could be. You remember that he was able to buy the building land he was negotiating for?"

Tarquin nodded. "On the evening of the day when you filled in as nurse at the kilns, you celebrated with dinner."

And by idiotically kissing him, with you looking on, Clare added silently, wondering if he remembered. "Yes," she agreed. "But he's just learned something that's quite disastrous to his plans –" As she went on to outline the problem she watched Tarquin, to see if he betrayed that he knew the facts. But he gave no sign. He listened, drawing on his cigar. "And so?" he invited when she finished.

"So? It means that he's facing the ruin of his hopes for the site. Isn't that enough?"

"He will be compensated for the land the authorities take. He must change his plans and build on the rest. In the end he shouldn't lose."

"But he can't build the type of house he wanted to build. Luxury homes and villas for retired people would never sell on the verges of a motorway."

"Then shouldn't he have looked into these dire possibilities before he closed on the purchase?"

"Oh, he knows about 'Caveat emptor' and all that. But would the Romans have made a saying of it or people have used it ever since, if a lot too many trusting buyers hadn't been caught by – " Clare checked in time on "fraudulent sellers" and substituted "their own rash enthusiasm? *I* think such people should be protected from themselves, not victimised and ruined, and afterwards refused advice!" she concluded in a flare of spirit against Tarquin's apparent indifference.

But she failed to goad him. "Suggesting that I'm refusing Bridgeman advice?" he asked. "I'd have said he should look to his solicitor for that."

"He doesn't trust his solicitor, I'm afraid."

"H'm. A pity. He should have changed him. What is the man's name?"

Clare told him and he nodded. "I know him," he said, non-committally, adding, "Meanwhile, such advice as I could give Bridgeman I remember offering him some time ago."

"In general terms, yes. But now all you can say in effect is 'I told you so'?"

"And you resent that for him?" Tarquin asked.

She looked straight at him. "I'm – disappointed," she said.

She saw his dark eyes glint. "And I'm surprised he should employ so passionately committed an advocate on so thin a case!" he retorted.

"Oscar *didn't* send me to you. I came myself," she replied with equal heat.

"Expecting what? Salvage for a scheme which no tyro as unversed as Bridgeman could hope to get off the ground unaided? If not, what?"

She gestured emptily. "Expecting nothing. Certainly no miracle rescue from his mistakes. But sympathy, perhaps advice. Something of the understanding and kindness you showed me when *I* was in trouble in a foreign country, at least partly through my – my blind folly by letting my impulses run ahead of my good sense as, in a way, Oscar has done. Not really *wanting* to probe the possible snags, either of us."

"I have no advice that isn't too late, and I'd be surprised if he would thank me for mere sympathy with his lack of business acumen," Tarquin parried. "And don't make his plight a parallel with yours. *He* could have taken guard, whereas, among other things which gave me the urge to help you, you were the victim of circumstances you couldn't possibly have foreseen."

"Your other reasons being that I was a girl, I suppose, and you thought you could help me by inviting me to be Eirene's companion," Clare suggested without much interest.

Tarquin flicked ash from his cigar, looked at its half-smoked length, then stubbed it out with a decisive turn of his wrist, before crossing the room towards the door.

"That you were a girl in distress, naturally. And that I saw advantage to us both in asking you to stay, yes. But I had another reason too," he said on his way.

"Another?"

"If you work on it, it may occur to you," he advised. "You'll excuse me now, if I go to see if there is anything I can do for Mama before she settles for the night?"

He left Clare to wish achingly that "working on it" could come up with the answer she wanted. Not, as he had surely meant, that he had, at the very outset, liked her and trusted her enough to invite her to Eirene, but that he had been man-to-woman attracted to her for herself; hadn't wanted to let her go . . . The impossible, impossible dream!

CHAPTER EIGHT

WHEN Eirene heard of the collapse of Oscar's land deal she was loud in her dismay and indignation. Clare had thought it discreet not to pass on to anyone Oscar's suspicions of Giorgio Fiore's duplicity. But Frank Bridgeman had no such scruples, and though Clare warned Eirene that Oscar had no proof, Eirene did not hesitate to voice them to anybody who would listen.

Clare knew she would not easily forget the evening when, finding she had a captive audience of the whole family at dinner, Eirene said suddenly, à propos of nothing, "I wish I thought any of you *cared* more than you seem to about Oscar Bridgeman's trouble. I mean, considering that he and Frank are friends of Clare's and mine, and that friends of yours have cheated them –" But there, her bald courage seeming to fail her, she broke off to scowl down at her plate, her twitching mouth mutinous.

The immediate effect was a charged silence. Lucio and Paolo Marini looked at each other, shrugging their shoulders and shaking their heads in mute bewilderment. Nicola, who in Clare's hearing had already been at the receiving end of Eirene's rancour on the subject, murmured, "*Cara mia,* you shouldn't –!" Signora Roscuro, in a characteristic use of her spectacles, first removed them for a scrutiny of Eirene's

141

lowered head, then replaced them and nodded to Tarquin in a gesture which said quite plainly, "Kindly deal with this."

Tarquin dealt with it. But not at once. He touched his lips with his table napkin and smoothed it with deliberation across his knees, as if he intended that the continuing silence should be broken by Eirene, not by him.

If so, he succeeded. Eirene looked up and round the table, then defied him with, "Well, it's true. Clare says she asked you if there were anything you could do for Oscar, and it's no use pretending she didn't tell you!"

"Tell me what?"

"Why, about Oscar being sure that Signor Fiore must have known about the motorway before he sold the land. And if he did, that's cheating, isn't it?"

"*If* he did, that's sharp practice," Tarquin agreed, his tone deceptively bland. "But if Bridgeman claims to be 'sure' without proof, then that's slander; pretty dangerous to say and equally dangerous to repeat."

"Not if it's true —" Eirene muttered.

Tarquin ignored her and turned his attention to Clare. "You knew that Bridgeman was harbouring this conviction, and you passed it on to Eirene?"

"I knew he had it, yes. But I didn't pass it on to her."

"Nor to me. Why not?"

"I suppose because I knew that if it weren't true, it was slanderous."

"And she certainly didn't tell me," interposed Eirene. "I had it from Frank."

"Who had it from his uncle, who expressed it to Clare, who seems to have been shrewd enough or to have had enough good taste to take it no further," Tarquin commented.

"Well, Clare is a nicer person than I am," Eirene admitted. "It doesn't make sense that Signor Fiore wouldn't have known about the motorway, but Clare didn't want to hurt you and

Nicola and Aunt Emilia by repeating it, considering that Jaquetta Fiore – according to herself – isn't far short of being one of the family! I mean, she is Nicola's friend, and you're going to marry her, aren't you? So naturally, even though Clare cares as much about Oscar and Frank as I do, she'd think it pretty bad form to blame Jaquetta's father to any of you. But I –"

Before she could go on Tarquin had cut in, "Exactly. Decent reticence and even common good manners aren't going to deter you from speaking your mind, are they? Though why you should link your ill-informed campaign for the Bridgemans to an impertinent tirade on our personal affairs, I'm at a loss to understand. Not to mention that I'd have thought that, as one of the family yourself and a guest in my mother's house, by now you might have grown at least as much grace and tact as Clare has. But no?"

"Yes, well –" For the first time appearing abashed, Eirene hesitated. But gathering herself she went on, "Well, it's as I've told you – Clare is good and kind, and too fond of you to – to soldier for Oscar as I know she must want to. We're just not made the same, that's all. Because, though I'm fond of you too, and you've all been kind, it just burns me up that nobody is really bothered about Oscar's being cheated out of his money and Frank out of the chance of a job. He's got to go back to England and find one. It's just all too bad, and – oh, but what's the *good*?" Putting into the last words all the woe of a frustrated child, Eirene pushed back her chair; in rising, stumbled over it, righted it with a savage twist, and fled from the room and the emotional havoc she had caused.

Nicola murmured, "Poor child, she has upset herself. I will go to her," and though Tarquin warned, "I doubt if you will be welcome," she went all the same.

The others made a show of finishing their dessert. The exchange between Eirene and Tarquin had been in English, and presently the uncles, who could not fully have understood its drift, excused themselves and left the table. Tarquin and his mother talked together in Italian – discussing Eirene's outburst, Clare knew, though they didn't invite any comment from her. But when she had finished eating and glanced at the Signora for permission to leave, Tarquin said, "Would you wait for me in the *salotto*? I'd rather like a word with you before I go home."

She had not to wait long for him to join her. When he did he asked abruptly, "Did you know Eirene was hatching such a grievance over the Bridgeman affair? I don't suppose you've encouraged her in it, but have you known she was taking it so to heart?"

"Yes, I've known," Clare admitted. "So has Nicola. We couldn't very well help it; she hasn't been able to leave it alone since she heard about it from Frank Bridgeman. And though she had no right to accuse you all as she did, I know she's pretty desolate about Oscar's having to send him back to England almost at once."

"Notwithstanding that she will be going back there herself in, at most, a month or two now?"

"But it's here that she's going to miss him, I think. She probably accepts that, in a couple of months or so, even the best of holiday friends may lose touch, and that's why she wants to keep him here while she's still here herself. On the other hand, if she thinks they may want to go on seeing each other, even two months apart must look like an age."

"Which all sounds like pretty self-interested thinking on her part," Tarquin commented.

"At sixteen-plus one *is* self-interested."

"Though at twenty-plus one can be detached enough and considerate enough of other people as to be almost self-effacing? Tell me, were you really concerned not to utter slander, or was Eirene right, that you wouldn't accuse

Jaquetta's father to me because of our involvement with them?"

"That, I think," Clare agreed. "Oscar had no proof, and I felt it wasn't fair."

"And supposing he had had sure proof, would you still have refrained?"

"Yes."

"Why?"

"Because, I suppose, one shouldn't accuse or criticise other people's close friends to them for one's own ends."

Tarquin nodded. "That's as I thought," he said. "But I suppose you consider I was hard on Eirene for not showing the same level of loyalty to us?"

"I thought you were too short with her, yes. She was obviously too sore to care what she said, and she's been coming to the boil for days. Besides," Clare added, "the way in which you held me up as a sample of control was neither very fair to her, nor true of me, considering how I accused you of withholding your advice from Oscar in this same connection."

"Though if I remember, you confined yourself to claiming disappointment in me. You didn't resort to insolent personalities, as Eirene did. No, you still get full marks for your restraint." Tarquin paused before adding, "Just now you used the phrase, 'for one's own ends'. Implying, I suppose, that Bridgeman's 'ends' in this business are also yours to a very fair degree?"

She hesitated, seeing her chance to discount the impression he might have gained from his witness of her impulsive kiss. But equally she mustn't be guilty of denying Oscar. She compromised with, "You could say that, I think. I do know a good deal about his ambitions, and if I hadn't been very worried for him in all this, I shouldn't have come to you to see if you could help."

"Only to go away empty-handed."

"There was nothing you could do. I accepted that," she murmured.

"Nor was there, as I saw it. It was too late. Meanwhile, you'll know of his plans now?"

"He is sending his nephew back to England, and staying on himself to try to find a buyer for the land at its greatly lowered value."

"And if he succeeds, what then for him?"

"I don't think he's looked ahead so far, and it probably must depend on the price he gets, before he can buy again. Do you want Eirene to apologise for all the wild accusations she flung at you?" Clare added.

"She could apologise to Mama and the others. As far as I'm concerned, she needn't trouble. But you could mention that she should have treated anything Jaquetta may have said about our relationship as the confidence it would have been."

Clare knew what he meant. "I think she was beside herself, but I'll do that," she promised. "Is that all?"

"For now." He went with her to the door when she rose. "You certainly work overtime at your conception of friendship," he remarked. "For instance, playing impassioned advocate in Bridgeman's already lost cause; getting into the skin of Eirene's immature reactions; deliberately refraining from scoring a point, out of consideration for our feelings. In other words, seeing your loyalties very clear and plain, and acting up to them."

Glowing at the implied praise, she looked up at him. "Well, surely that's what friendship is all about?" she parried.

"Though what a pity to restrict your talent for it only to the support of your friends!"

For a moment she was puzzled. Then she understood, and the glow faded. She said, "You are reminding me, aren't you, that I once told you I was disillusioned with family ties, that I should be cautious of getting tangled with them in future?"

"Exactly. You let me stress your resolve with our proverb about the smoke and the flame, claiming you had nothing to offer nor wanted anything of anyone who was hedged in by family obligations. Fair enough comment, reminding you, I thought, if you are of the same sentiments still?"

"And supposing I don't still think like that?"

His tone different now, warmer, he said, "I'd like to believe that. But if you don't, since when?"

"Since – since I've known your family – the way you all belong, the sort of pride you take *in* belonging to each other and to all your past."

His brows went up in question. "I declare, you have been allowing Uncle Paolo to brainwash you!"

She shook her head. "No, though we've talked a lot. No, when I told you I envied you San Marino I meant I envied everything you have here – your work, your people, your – future; the way your family will go on."

"I see. But you didn't make me understand so at the time. And why stop short at envy? If you cared to, couldn't you make the place and a life here your own?"

"Not in the same way. It's not my country, as it is yours. I don't belong, my work isn't here, and when Eirene goes home I shall go too, and take it up again as soon as I can."

"So for all your change of heart, no idle lotus-eating here for you?"

She smiled faintly. "I'm afraid not. I must go back to England. It was only infatuation and a mirage of wishful thinking that brought me out to Italy in the first place, and a good fortune I didn't deserve, your finding work for me and giving me a home here."

"And you are determined that you won't make capital out of mere fate? Very, *very* laudable!" Now he was ironic, but his hand went out to her arm, staying her as she was about to

147

turn away. "All the same, will you give me one promise – that before you decide irrevocably on your going, we shall talk again?"

Fleetingly she realised that it was the first time he had asked anything of her without the assumption that she must agree; the first time he hadn't made almost an order of a request; the first time he had seemed to allow that she might say No.

Willingly, gladly, she said, "Of course, yes."

By the next day the troubled atmosphere caused by Eirene's outburst had been dispelled by her unstinted apology for it to the Signora, who rewarded her with a magnanimous kiss and a regal "We shall think no more about it, child. When one is young and ardent, the tongue often says too much" – which dismissed the subject and helped to restore Eirene to a sunnier mood.

She asked for, and got, permission to see Frank frequently before his departure for England and she invited him once or twice to the Casa, after warning him, she told Clare, against mentioning Oscar's disaster to any member of the family – an order which he obeyed to the letter and gained the Signora's approval as an "admirable and modest young man" whom she was "happy to receive" for Eirene, she claimed.

Nicola was approaching the end of her pregnancy with the same serene confidence as she had brought to it all along. "Naturally", she confided to Clare and Eirene, her husband wanted a boy baby, but for her it was "this way or that; a boy or a girl – no matter" A *bambino* was a *bambino*, and as long as hers arrived on time, whole and entire and healthily hungry, she was not troubled.

It was her husband, Marco, who arrived first, anxious and fussing – When would the nurse move in? (Nicola was to be confined at the Casa). Could the doctor be alerted conveniently, day or night? Had everything, but everything, been prepared for the layette? Was Nicola comfortable? Happy? Too warm? Too cold? Hungry or thirsty? Tired? Nobody, Nicola chuckled complacently, would suppose that it was his nerve and his skill which edged huge tonnages of oil tanker into the world's narrowest of docking berths, when he could not trust her to produce a baby without his help! Or was it, perhaps, that it was his minute attention to detail which made him a tanker pilot of the first rank? One could look at it either way, could one not?

Spring came to San Marino in the last days of January, early that year and bursting with life.

Now it was not necessary to buy mimosa in the market; the wattle shrubs in the gardens and the streets were all over yellow with buttons which opened into floss. The boughs of flowering cherry were heavy with fattening buds, and climbing roses on sheltered house-walls dared to put out blossoms while their leaves were still winter-dormant. The skies were a clear pale blue and the strengthening warmth of the sun brought down mists at night – mists which cleared fast from San Marino's peaks, more slowly from the plains, so that, seen from below on such a morning, its walls and buildings seemed to rise up out of nothing and to float upon cloud – the ramparts and towers of a pantomime transformation scene, no less.

The date of Eirene's return to England was still indefinite, but her mother, who was already back in their London home, would be sending for her very shortly. Eirene was less elated at the prospect than Clare had expected, and Clare could only surmise that she hadn't been told of the success or failure of her parents' trial separation, and was fearing the worst. Her reply to Clare's tentative question was that "Daddy wasn't at home at present – only Mummy", and that he had been on a business trip to Yugoslavia when she had last heard from him. She confided nothing more, and Clare did not press her. She asked Nicola instead if she knew the circumstances to which Eirene would be returning. But Nicola did not. Mama, she said, was waiting to hear when Eirene was to be recalled, and they could only pray – Nicola, ever the optimist! – that there would be some "happy news" then. For Clare the uncertainty meant so many days counted and savoured one by one. The months which Eirene had seen as a prison sentence had flown too quickly for her. There was loneliness and a time-for-forgetting ahead. But for the moment she had San Marino's sunshine, and the bracing security of the Casa and Tarquin's goodwill, if not his love, and she was almost content.

Frank had delayed his going in order to apply for one or two jobs which he had failed to get, and on the day of his flight out Oscar, Clare and Eirene arranged to see him off at the airport. The two girls went out by bus; Oscar and Frank met them in the car-park, and Frank at once claimed Eirene's company for the hour before his flight was called.

"Where shall we meet you?" Clare wanted to know. But Frank said vaguely, "Oh – around," and Oscar took her arm in an urgent grip. "Let them go," he muttered. "It's the last time they'll have together, this side of the English Channel, and I must see you alone too. There has been an extraordinary development, and Frank doesn't know."

He found a table in a sunny corner of the outside balcony and ordered *cappuccinos*, his own cup of which, however, he pushed aside. Clare found his manner strange; neither elated nor depressed, but nervous, as if he didn't know what to make of the "development" himself.

She had to prompt him. "Well? What has happened? Something to do with the land?"

He looked beyond her, fingering his chin. "Yes."

"You've been able to sell it again?"

150

"I – had an anonymous feeler some days ago. Through my solicitor, from someone who would only make himself known if I agreed to parley on some perhaps rather unorthodox terms which he would put to me."

"And you said –?"

"I questioned 'unorthodox'. I didn't know what that meant, and nor did my man. But as I couldn't lose anything by talking, I said Yes, and he made an appointment for us at his office. And then came the shock, Clare. The prospect was Tarquin Roscuro!"

"*Tarquin?*"

"Himself. And he lost no time in stating his terms. Unorthodox terms? I'll say they were! They weren't financial terms at all. They were conditions I must agree to, if he were going to buy."

"But I don't understand!" puzzled Clare. "Why should he be interested? He's not in land dealing. Why should he want it?"

"That's what I asked, and he said he could use it for warehouses and showrooms for Roscuro ceramics – giving tourists a kind of foretaste of what they could buy if they went up to San Marino. And the fact of the motorway would be no disadvantage to commercial property like that; quite the reverse, in fact."

"But his conditions? What were they?"

"Ah." Oscar compressed his lips. "They emerged. Naturally I assumed he would offer the cut price I could expect, in view of the motorway's going through. But before I could suggest the figure I had been advised to ask, he asked me what I had paid Fiore for it. And when I told him, he said 'I'll give you that – on my terms. They being that you go back to England and invest in land speculation there, not here.' "

Clare gasped. "He had no right to put such a bargain to you! How dared he? The – the *arrogance* of it – thinking he could

151

order your future so! You didn't agree, of course?"

Oscar drew his cup towards him, took a sip or two of cold coffee. "I told him I would seriously consider it," he said.

"Oscar, you *didn't?*"

"I did. I had to. I did tell him they were most peculiar conditions and that he couldn't force them on me. To which he agreed blandly enough that he knew he couldn't. I was free to take them or leave them, as I pleased, but that his offer was conditional upon my accepting them. And in the end I did."

Clare shook her head in despair. "But why? *Why?*"

"Why did I agree? Or why did he put them to me?"

"Both, I suppose –"

"Well, as to his motives, he forestalled me by saying he had reasons which were not for discussion. And why I agreed was because – well, I realised he wasn't asking so much of me after all. You see, Clare, I was already halfway to the brink of a decision to call it a day, businesswise, here in Italy. And Roscuro's offer just pushed me over the edge."

"But you had ambitions out here. You thought you could succeed!"

"So I had. So I did. But the case has altered, hasn't it? Without this offer, I can't help but drop two-thirds of my capital. I couldn't buy elsewhere as I hoped I could, and I hope I'm honest enough to admit that I've been had for a sucker; I'm a babe in the wood, with my head covered in dead leaves, and it's time I got out."

"All the same, Tarquin *bought* you!" Clare accused.

"No – I let him buy me. He may have seen it as an ultimatum. *I* saw it as a heaven-sent way out. With my capital restored, I can almost certainly put it to good use in England. Italy, I see now, was something of a pipe-dream. Not that I regret one moment of my time here– for the same reason that I'm spoiling now to get back to England – the reason being you,

Clare. You, here by chance for our meeting; you, back in England when your job with the Roscuros ends. And that makes sense enough to me. Does it make any to you?"

She answered that obliquely. "It's practical sense, I suppose. And it will be pleasant, looking forward to meeting in England –"

His head went to rest on hers. "Ultimately, more than 'meeting', Clare – please?" he begged. But she was spared having to answer that as, at the far end of the balcony she espied Eirene's gamine head appearing above the top step of the stairway leading to it.

"The others – they're coming over," she said to Oscar. "You say you haven't said anything to Frank about all this?"

"No, and I'm not going to. When the time comes, I can find him another job with me in England, if he wants to join me. But for the moment, while he hasn't one, he could accuse me of – ratting," Oscar said quickly as Frank and Eirene drew near.

Clare looked at him, half tempted to query. "Well?", but she bit back the cruelty in time. It wasn't his fault. He needed his ill-spent money back, and he had the courage to know when he was beaten by circumstance. No, it was Tarquin – despising Oscar's incompetence, bribing him for some quirk of reasoning best known to himself, flaunting his willingness to pay, to prove his theory that Oscar had been out of his depth from the start – it was Tarquin who had ratted on her faith in his integrity, in the kindness she had had at his hands.

It was Tarquin being as ruthless as Jaquetta had once said of him; as hard as he had shown himself when she had gone to him to plead Oscar's cause. Now she wasn't disappointed. She was angry, both angry and frustrated in her urge to protest, for Tarquin was in Rome on business, and she had several days in which to wonder at the contradiction of loving him, yet being outraged by her glimpse of his feet of clay.

She could only suppose that it was possible to give your heart, yet still to retain your sense of values; to see the loved one with dispassion, and so – perhaps – to be cured of a hopeless loving in the end.

This time, she decided, she could not rely on chance to provide a tête-à-tête occasion for her with Tarquin. For the brief time she would need to say to him what she had to, she must ensure that they were alone. At the Casa, where he arrived and left at unspecified times, except for his morning visit to his mother, this was not possible, and flouting San Marino convention as it might, to call at his villa was her only choice. And in any case, from the moment of her appearance on his doorstep she meant to leave him in no doubt of the absence of any romantic undertones to her call. San Marino's ears need do no interested pricking over her lack of a chaperon.

But appearing on his doorstep was not so easy . . . When she knew she would find him at home after his return from Rome she had braced herself, only to retreat more than once from the ordeal of facing him, and when she had at last climbed the little flight of steps to his door, her heart was thumping thickly almost in her throat before he opened to her.

His welcome, cordial as it was, held surprise, as she had known it would. He held the door wide for her, showed her into the room she remembered from the night of the Pallium contest, and indicating a chair for her, said, "This is pleasant. What can I do for you? Something? Or nothing – if it's just a friendly call?"

His sense of the local proprieties must know it wasn't, she told herself, and she shook her head, ignoring the chair. "I'm afraid it isn't meant to be pleasant," she said, and watched his expression change.

"No?"

The unhelpful monosyllable was daunting to the lines she had rehearsed, as from a script. Now she was fumbling for words. "I – haven't spoken to Nicola or the Signora about this. I came straight to you," she said. "To tell you – that is, to ask you to release me at – at this amount of notice only, from my contract as Eirene's companion. I – I could leave just as soon as it would be convenient for you to let me go."

He looked at her, saying nothing. Then he pointed again to the chair. "I think you had better sit down," he said, making an order of it.

She sat. He remained standing, supporting himself against a table-edge, arms folded. Looking down at her from that superior height, "Why?" he asked.

She re-found some of her courage. "Because I feel that from now on, I couldn't work in any accord with you or for you. And I hope I have only to remind you that Oscar Bridgeman is a friend of mine, for you to understand why not," she said.

"Oscar Bridgeman. Of course." He nodded. "But could you make the connection with your post with us a shade more clear? I take it he has told you of my offer to relieve him of his white elephant. But what has that to do with your reluctance to honour your contract with us to its end?"

She avoided his eyes. "I think you should know," she said. "The connection is that *I* have no right to continue to work for you, while I consider that *you* had no right – utterly no right! – to impose the conditions that you did. They were monstrous. And – and irrelevant. And unfair."

"You mean the clause which stipulated his return to England?"

"Of course. That one."

"Though I couldn't force it on him. And he agreed to it readily enough."

"Well, what did you expect? He needed the money too badly! But that doesn't make your demanding it of him very far short of – blackmail." She had planned to use the ugly

155

word, and now it was out, not to be recalled.

Tarquin accepted it in silence for a moment. Then he said, "Nothing of the sort. It was a gentleman's agreement which Bridgeman was free to take or leave, as he chose. He took it."

"And you imposed it for reasons at which it isn't hard to guess!" Clare accused.

A shrug answered that. "I'm a business man. When I know I want something, I bargain for it on my terms, and in this case my reasons had value enough to me."

"But if you had *merely* wanted the land for showrooms on the highway, you could probably have got it at whatever was its market price. No, I'm pretty sure you dangled the carrot of the full price Oscar had paid, just to show him up; to label him as the incompetent you've always thought him; to make sure he gave you the satisfaction of saying 'I told you so' by his accepting your bribe to him to admit his failure and get out. I think you needed to humiliate him, in order to prove yourself right."

"I see. My motives laid out, analysed and duly judged as bribery and corruption? It hadn't occurred to you, I suppose, that without some such attractive persuasion as my offer, Bridgeman might have continued to muddle on here, rather than return to England where he must know he would have more success?" Tarquin asked.

"I don't think he would have stayed. He has learned his lesson at other hands than yours. But even if he had decided to stay, whose business would that be but his?" she retorted.

"Except," Tarquin reminded her, "that he allowed me to make it mine. I hadn't to twist his arm, and we parted in reasonable accord. And that being settled, why his returning home should rouse you to such ire I am at a loss to understand. Weren't you insisting only very recently that nothing would keep you from going back to England yourself before long?"

She looked up at him. "But not 'before long' now. At

156

once, please. As soon as you will let me go."

He straightened then, took the few steps to the window and spoke to her over his shoulder. Making every word count, he said, "Which I have no intention of doing, I'm afraid."

Staring at his back she gasped, "You can't keep me here against my will!"

"I mean to – against a silly impulse to leave which you will have to forget for the moment."

"Now you are twisting *my* arm!" Clare was near to panic. "And how *can* I stay after – all this? With this ill-feeling between us?"

He turned back to face her. He said, "It's a rancour that is only on your side, not on mine, and I must ask you to control it in front of my family. And to enlarge on that – Nicola, for one, has grown fond of you, and Eirene, for another, still depends on your companionship. And so, at this stage of her health, I am not having Nicola upset by your leaving, nor Eirene deserted before she leaves San Marino herself. In short, you will remain bound by your contract with us. Do I make myself clear?"

On the down-beat of a long breath, "Perfectly," said Clare.

"And you will agree to stay?"

Her chin went up. "I'm not brawling with you over it. I must."

"Good. And I hope I'm going to be able to hold you to another promise you made me – to talk with me again about your plans, before you do leave San Marino?"

This at least she could deny him – and herself – the bittersweet she had envisaged in the prospect. She stood up and on her way to the door, said, "Not that one. After this I can't imagine wanting to discuss anything that is personal to me with you again."

He opened the door for her, and then the outer door to the street below. "Nor I with you? You shouldn't be too sure of that, I think," he countered as he saw her down the steps, his hand gentle under her elbows, for all the world as if he were speeding a parting friend.

He was inexplicable! She had expected him to be angry, as outraged with her as she had felt with him; even that he would not allow her to state her case before throwing her out. Instead he had been controlled and authoritative; returning not the soft answer, but the firm cool one to her wrath. And at the end, almost melting it with his reminder of the promise she had given him so willingly. Almost – but not quite. It was too late to yield to loving him again without question. That she could not afford.

CHAPTER NINE

IT was Eirene who first brought the astonishing news.

As she told the story to Clare, who was the first person she encountered on her return to the Casa one morning, she had been passing the Fiores' villa when her scooter's engine had stuttered and failed, and she had had to stop and change its sparking-plug – a job which need take only a few minutes, once she had unearthed a new plug and a spanner from the clutter of things she carried around in her saddle-bag. Head down, rummaging, she had just located both when she noticed the girl, in the mini-skirted uniform and saucy pillbox hat of an exclusive Rimini boutique, who had alighted from the delivery van which had parked at the kerb, just behind Eirene's machine.

The girl balanced two dress-boxes between her spread hands and her chin as she paused to speak to the boy driver. Eirene had heard her say, "I may have to go in while she looks at these. So wait for me, will you?" before she elbowed open the villa's gate and approached the front door.

Meanwhile Eirene got to work on the offending plug, though failing to unscrew it at several turns of the spanner. The delivery girl had not come straight back; the boy watched Eirene's abortive attempts for some minutes, then slowly extricated himself from his driving seat and came forward to offer his help.

"Was I grateful?" Eirene demanded rhetorically of Clare.

"He had the wretched thing off and the other screwed in, and the engine kicked over before I could decide between offering him a tip or smiling at him all over my face. But just then his girl-friend came back, still carrying the dress-boxes and looking – well, flattened is the only word for it. The boy seemed to guess what I was at, when I fumbled for some cash, and he waved his arms and shook his head to show he didn't want any, and the girl just stood and said, 'She isn't there.'"

"He echoed that, and said, 'She is out?' And the girl said, 'Not out. She is no longer there. The Signore and the Signorina, both gone away. Suddenly, last night. The woman who answered the door to me said she didn't know where they had gone. They had left no address, and she was only the house-keeper, left to close up the house.' And what about *that*?" concluded Eirene, eyeing Clare for her reaction.

Clare gasped. "Gone *away*? They can't have! Not like that!"

Eirene nodded confirmation of her superior information. "Seems so. In a moonlight flit, what's more!"

"They wouldn't," Clare denied the possibility. "Signor Fiore is rich – look at that villa! And Jaquetta's clothes and her car. And his business in Rimini. He wouldn't just walk out of that overnight. Besides, someone here – Tarquin, for instance, would know, and we should have heard that they were leaving."

"Should we – you and I, I mean – if they wanted to keep it dark?" queried Eirene sagely. "And if it is a moonlight flit, would Tarquin, especially, want to advertise it?"

Out of her depth in bewilderment, Clare agreed dully, "I suppose not," her reason telling her how absurd were Eirene's conclusions from the story, her will wanting to believe they were true and that Jaquetta Fiore had indeed removed herself from the immediate scene without notice of her going.

Clare asked Eirene, "What happened next?"

"Oh – well, this boy and the girl got back into the van. I

thanked him again, and he did and said a sort of Italian 'Delighted. Any time – ' and they drove off and I came back to tell you. Now I suppose we wait to hear what the family knows – if anything," said Eirene.

They had not to wait long. After visiting his mother, Tarquin had left as usual, but he returned an hour later, and he, Nicola and her husband and the Signora were closeted together for a long time. He did not stay for lunch, and it was Nicola who enlightened the two girls.

"Tarquin brought some shocking news," she said. "Almost unbelievable. Mama and I do not know what to think, but it seems that some of it was no news to Tarquin. It is about Signor Fiore's business. It is in bad legal and money trouble; he has closed his office, owing his staff their salaries and wages, and – though this took Tarquin completely by surprise – the Signore has disappeared overnight from his villa, taking Jaquetta with him and telling no one where they were going." Nicola broke off, sighing. "Oh dear! Such a thing to happen! Such a disgrace for them, and such a shock for their friends. For us. For Tarquin – "

Eirene nodded. "We knew they had left very suddenly."

"*You* knew? How?"

Eirene recounted how, and said she had told Clare, who couldn't believe it either.

"But sadly it is true," said Nicola. "Though not for long, Tarquin had heard rumours of difficulties, and yesterday it came into the open – that Giorgio Fioro has been using the firm's money, and falsifying accounts and cheating clients of their rights for more than a year." Nicola sounded distressed as she added, "And of course we have to question how much Jaquetta may have known; how much she was involved, and why she did not persuade her father that he must not run away. Instead, she has gone with him. And that looks bad."

Clare sympathised, "I am so sorry. She was your friend."

161

"Tarquin's too. At one time I think Mama hoped – And I confess I thought they might marry. But I have doubted it for some time now. He has been – correct with Jaquetta lately, but no more."

Eirene put in bluntly, "Well, she told *me* once that they were as good as engaged. And that was why – " she stopped, flushing. "Well, you know the rather awful things I said that night at dinner. About none of you caring that Oscar and Frank were being cheated, and – "

"But we don't remember them against you, *cara mia*," Nicola smiled. "And though you were so angry with us, perhaps you had cause. Perhaps you were wiser than you knew, and perhaps we have been the blind ones – who can tell?"

At which point Marco Bernini, shadowing his wife as always, ruled that she had had enough worry for one day; that she must think of the *bambino* and must rest. Whereupon, protest as Nicola might that neither she nor the *bambino* were made of Venetian glass, he shepherded her to her room and an enforced siesta.

"Wiser than I knew!" chuckled Eirene. "*There's* a quaint way of saying 'How right you were, chum.' But it looks as if Oscar was, about his being cheated over his land. It's all rather exciting, isn't it? I've never known an embezzler before. What do you suppose Nicola meant, that Tarquin had been 'correct' with Jaquetta? That the idea of marrying her had gone cold on him and he was keeping her at arm's length? It wouldn't be so funny, though, supposing he came over all chivalrous and married her for pity, now her father is in disgrace. And I suppose, wherever they've gone, they'll be traced some time?"

Clare supposed so too, and wished she could share Eirene's extrovert interest in the happening. It was odd, she thought, that she, the outsider, should feel involved with the proud

Roscuros' betrayed loyalties, where Eirene, one of them, should see their dilemma only in terms of its possibly exciting development. If only she were in a position now to be able to say to Tarquin, "I'm so sorry," and mean it, as she had done to Nicola! But now she could not; he would not give her the opportunity. Whenever they met now he was polite but distant, while she often contrived to address him "through" someone else. She wondered whether anyone had noticed how extremely correct – in Nicola's phrase – their relationship now was!

He did not revisit the Casa that day, and at dinner, when Eirene seemed set upon a cosy rehash of the scandal, the Signora ruled in her most imperious manner, "We shall talk of pleasant matters over our meal, child. The more unsavoury ones can wait."

"As if," Eirene grumbled to Clare later "supposing you let them wait long enough, they disappear!" But at dinner she bowed to the edict, talked "baby" to Nicola and her husband, and teased the uncles and came no nearer to the forbidden subject than to commiserate with Clare about Oscar's departure for England the next day.

By now she knew, as did the others, that Tarquin had purchased the land, and for what purpose. She had wondered at Oscar's decision to go home, but Clare did not enlighten her as to Tarquin's part in that, and after her first surprise she argued to her own satisfaction that, having originally involved Frank, Oscar probably felt he still owed Frank a living. Which was pretty decent of Oscar, and justice for Frank and the promise of some pleasant get-togethers when they all – she and Clare too – were back in England. She was looking forward to it. And wasn't Clare?

Later – much later, when it had all happened – Clare was to look back with hindsight and wonder that the cataclysmic day which followed that of the Fiores' strategic departure

163

should have dawned like any other of the ordinary days which rolled unremarked throughout their length until dark. It should, her after-knowledge thought, have been heralded by – well, by something; by some sign in the calendar; some forewarning that it would be as different from its yesterday as Midsummer Eve from New Year. For it wasn't only with her fate that it sported; its currents galvanised other lives than hers. Yet afterwards there had been no one to claim even, "I had a *feeling* about this day," or "My thumbs pricked," or "I knew in my bones – ". For them all it had begun just like any other.

Clare woke to its morning and looked at her plans for it. In the afternoon she was going to see Oscar off at the airport. She had promised him she would, but she saw it as an ordeal for them both. She knew he would want to see her when she went back to England herself, and though they had not met since the day Frank had left, in their talks on the telephone his hope of making her more than a friend was always implicit. She didn't want to hurt him, but she must.

The forenoon was a blank, to be filled with anything which came up. It was a lovely day; she would wait to see what Eirene wanted to do with it. It was good not to be a corner in the Eirene-Clare-Jaquetta triangle any more. Would there be any development in the Fiore affair? How was Tarquin taking it? She wished she had enough of his confidence to know or to guess, and to dare to sympathise.

Nicola's midwife was already installed at the Casa. She was an authoritative little woman, whom long experience had taught to be short with anxious husbands; who always spoke of Nicola or to her in the plural "we" and who radiated a confidence that all had better go well with the birth – or else! She was crossing the hall as Clare went downstairs that morning, and announced without being asked that "we were very well indeed this morning", and that "there would be no trouble

164

for us when our time came." After sharing this information between Clare and Tarquin, who came in at that moment, she hurried off to the kitchen quarters to resume her daily battle for her superior status over Anna and the maids.

The astonishing day began its surprises when Tarquin stopped Clare on her way to the breakfast room. "You'll have heard that Signor Fiore has absconded from his house and his business has closed?" he asked.

"Yes, Nicola told us. I'm – very sorry." Clare hadn't found it too difficult to say, after all. But Tarquin rejected it.

"Don't waste your sympathy," he said. "The facts show that for far too long he has duped too many victims – and almost certainly Oscar Bridgeman among them. Which means I owe you both an apology, and I'm making it."

Disarmed by the unexpected tribute, Clare asked, "You mean your accusing Oscar of professional bungling and your refusal to advise him through me? But when I came to you, you didn't know the facts, and he only suspected he had been cheated. And when he does learn the truth, he'll have nothing to hold against you."

"But you will, still?"

She looked away. "That was about something quite different, and I don't expect Oscar to understand my feelings about that."

"Nor did he ever, I'd say, considering the ease with which he accepted my conditions." Tarquin went on, "Anyway, he heard the details about the Fiore affair yesterday. I wanted him told before he left for England. He'll be ringing you with the news, I expect."

Clare said, "Probably not, now. He's flying out this afternoon, and I'm seeing him off at the airport."

Tarquin's brows lifted. "So soon? And when now do you propose to follow him?"

Startled, she drew a sharp breath. "You refused to allow me to consider going until – !"

His voice cut across hers. "And now I'm saying you may go when you please – *after* we have had that final talk which you promised me. And the sooner the better. What time do you need to be down at the airport?"

She told him and he nodded. "Then I'll drive you, leave you to make your partings, and we'll talk before I bring you back. Agreed?"

"But that – my promising to talk . . . to listen was before – all that's happened since!" she protested. "You can't want to say any of the same things – help me, advise me, persuade me to stay in Italy – as you did then!"

"I still have to talk and you have to listen," he insisted. "I shall call for you this afternoon. Meanwhile, you haven't answered my question. When do you want to leave?"

As bewildered by his release of her as a life-sentenced prisoner flung without warning upon the world, she said, "If I may, I'd like to stay now until Eirene goes home."

"Then you have changed your mind about running out prematurely? Why?"

"Because – well, I've realised I had no right to make an issue about it over Oscar's affairs."

"Nor had you," he agreed. "I knew that, if you didn't. Which in part was why I refused to let you go on any other terms than mine. For the rest –"

She nodded quickly. "I know. You wouldn't have Nicola upset nor Eirene abandoned, you said."

"That too. But I also determined that you shouldn't go until we had our talk, and at the time you were in no mood for it."

She looked up at him. "And you think I may be now?" she asked, and as soon the words were out, wished they hadn't sounded arch.

Head at an angle, lips thrust forward, he considered her face. "Chastened enough to listen to reason? Yes, I hope so," he said.

Reason. Advice. Well-meant warnings. Mere crumbs to her hunger. But that he cared enough to want to offer them sent a prickle of nervous excitement along her spine.

Later she was glad that fate allowed her an hour or two of looking forward to a rendezvous which was not to take place. Buoyed by her thought of it, up to a certain point in time, she enjoyed her morning.

Nicola did not appear as usual after breakfast. Nurse Lorenz bustled upstairs and down, her face pursed and important, and Marco Bernini, forbidden Nicola's room, roamed the house, chain-smoking and seeking reassurance from everyone he met.

Nicola was in the first stages of labour. He knew it. So why hadn't the doctor been called? La Lorenz, as he called her, had told him there was plenty of time yet. But how far could be trust her? How could she *tell*?

Eirene didn't know the answer to that one. Nor did either of the uncles, both of whom went to ground in their own sanctums, effacing themselves from a domestic crisis of which, Lucio having had no family and Paolo being a bachelor, they had little experience. Clare, recalling her days of duty on the gynaecological ward in hospital, told Marco that almost certainly there was no need for the doctor until Nurse Lorenz decided to call him, and the Signora countered her son-in-law's questions by putting one of her own. How many babies since time began *had* made successful debuts without a doctor to hold them by the hand, did Marco suppose? Or even – thousands, millions, trillions of them – without benefit of a nurse?

"Remember the Christ Child Himself," she ordered grandiloquently, "and be thankful that your La Lorenz can be assumed to know what she is about!"

Eirene did her best by Marco by inviting him to a game of

Scrabble in Italian, and Clare walked into the town to do some shopping for Anna, who suspected Nurse Lorenz of all kinds of liberties in her kitchen when she was absent from it.

Clare had finished all she had to do and had paused, a short way up the steepest street in the town, momentarily dazzled by the glint of the sun on the metal of a motor-bicycle being ridden down the hill at speed . . . at breakneck speed, out of control, and as Clare held her breath, fearing it must crash, she recognised Eirene's scooter and glimpsed Eirene's terror-stricken face.

Everything happened within seconds.

Clare glanced behind her at the continuing slope downhill; calculated the dangerous speed the machine would have gathered by the time it reached it; noted the gradual uphill climb of a street turning with which she stood level and which should be a simple nearside turn for the girl to make. If she did it, the very gradient would check her speed – Upon the instant of decision, Clare signalled. "Turn right!"; Eirene seemed to understand and obeyed. But by then her handlebars were wobbling wildly; the small wheels skidded and slid on the rough of the roadway; the crash was inevitable as the machine hit a wall and rebounded, throwing Eirene from the saddle as if she were a rag doll, and itself crumpling, its engine dying in a final roar of protest.

Clare ran, her breath coming in hard sobs from her throat. It was her fault! She should have known Eirene couldn't make the turn at that speed. If she had allowed her to go straight on, perhaps – ?

Eirene lay very still, her crash helmet knocked awry, her face bleeding from pocks made by fragments of thrown-up gravel from the road, her body twisted, one leg still pinned under the back wheel of the scooter.

Clare knelt beside her. People gathered, shouting, jostling, crossing themselves and murmuring, "*La povera ragazza!*" in irresolute pity. Clare pulled herself together, demanded of someone, "Call the police – an ambulance!" and knelt again, as Eirene opened her eyes, whimpered, and shut them again.

After that the police were there, clearing the crowd, asking of Clare, "How? " "Who?" "You know her, *signorina*?" "Where from?" and uttering "Ah's" of respectful comprehension at mention of the Casa and Eirene's connection with it. The ambulance came and Clare and a policeman rode in it with Eirene to the hospital. Eirene was wheeled away into the "casualty" ward for "observation" and to Clare fell the task of ringing the Casa to tell what had happened.

It was Marco who answered the telephone – a Marco so excited that he said neither the usual "*Pronto*", nor asked who was speaking before he burst out with, "Yes, yes – a boy! A fine boy – just five minutes ago, and the doctor not here – imagine that! So timely – your happening to call to enquire; the first call we have had!" and only then paused to ask who was on the line; whom he should tell Nicola had been the first of her friends to hear the good news that she had a son and he, a Bernini heir – ?

In as calm a voice as she could summon, Clare told him, "It's Clare Yorke here, Signor Bernini, and I'm so very glad about the baby. But I didn't ring about that. It's about Eirene, I'm afraid. She has had an accident and she is in hospital. She –"

He interrupted then. "*Eirene?* But she was here! We were playing that board game to pass the time for me, and when I had no more cigarettes, she went to buy me some, since I couldn't leave, you understand?"

"Yes, well – " said Clare. "She went on her scooter and must have lost control of it, or perhaps the brakes failed. It crashed at the corner of the Via Spoleto and she is hurt, I don't know how badly yet. But I was there; I saw it happen, and I am at the hospital now." Her voice shook as she added,

"You won't tell Nicola, of course. But someone ought to know. The Signora, perhaps, if you could break it gently to her. Or Tarquin, if you could get in touch with him at the kilns or wherever he might be."

"Yes, yes, Tarquin, of course. He must know." Distressed, Marco added, "I should not have sent the child on my stupid errand. I am to blame – "

Clare cut in, "No, it was my fault."

"Yours, Signorina Clare? How – !"

But Clare was listening to the rustling and murmurs which followed at his end of the line, and then she heard Tarquin's voice, incisive, curt, "Tarquin here. Clare? What's all this about Eirene?"

She repeated all she had told Marco, and was about to admit her part in the crash when he cut her short. "And you are at the hospital now, yourself? Then stay there, and I'll be over." He rang off, and she waited, knowing, even in her agony of mind, a measure of peace in feeling she had his taut strength to rely upon, his lead to follow.

His arrival coincided with that of the Casualty surgeon, coming to give his report. Tarquin closed the door of the room upon Clare and took it alone. Coming back, he nodded dismissal of the policeman who was still sitting with Clare, and told her, "They can't tell the full extent of the injuries yet. Externally there are those cuts on her face and her left elbow is broken. That has been set, and she is under sedation. All her other limbs are sound, but there is a chance of some internal injury from crushed ribs, though there is no sign of this at present."

Claire moistened her dry lips. "You mean there's no haemorrhage?"

"They hope not. Nor any external wound, except her cut face. But they won't know until she has been X-rayed, and they are keeping her here, of course."

"Yes. Do you – do you think I might see her?" Clare hesitated.

Tarquin shook his head. "Better not," he advised kindly. "She probably isn't a pretty sight, and may be too far under to know you. We'll keep in touch, but I'm taking you home now. There's nothing more we can do for Eirene here until we have more news."

Her nod acquiesced dumbly and she went with him after a backward lingering glance at the corridor along which they had wheeled Eirene away.

In the car Tarquin explained, "I had just looked in at the Casa for news of Nicola, and found Marco at the telephone. Between his own news and yours, he was pretty incoherent, but I did gather that you were there when Eirene crashed. Were you out together? And what did Marco mean by claiming he was to blame? I didn't wait to hear."

Clare said quickly, "He didn't mean anything. He wasn't. And we weren't together. I had gone into the town alone, and as Signor Bernini didn't want to leave the house, Eirene went to buy cigarettes for him. I was on my way back when she was coming down here," – the car was mounting the same hill now – "going at a speed I realised she couldn't control, and – "

"Why did she attempt the turn into the Via Spoleto?"

There was a beat of silence. Then: "Because – Because I signalled her to. I thought – " Clare's voice broke and aware of Tarquin's swift, compassionate glance, she was ashamed.

He said. "I see. But leave it for now." To her surprise he pulled up outside his own villa, and in answer to her look of enquiry, said, "The Casa has enough to occupy it just now, and I made Marco promise to hold his tongue for the moment about Eirene. *I* want to break it to Mama. And you need a rest and steadying before I advise you to keep your date. You can take it easy for an hour and have luncheon with me."

171

Clare's jaw dropped. "My – date? What – ?" Then she remembered. "Oh, Oscar! At the airport! But – but I can't go now!"

"Why not?" Tarquin got out of the car, helped her out and led the way into his house. "When you've rested and had something to eat, we'll go back to the Casa. I'll see Mama, and you can get ready to – "

"No!" She turned to him in panic. "I can't go. Not today, Not now. Not while Eirene – Don't make me, *please*. Oscar will understand!"

"*Will* he?"

"Yes, yes, I know he will. It – it wasn't as important as all that, my seeing him off, and I'd never forgive myself if Eirene – got worse . . . or anything while I was away, and you were too. No, please – I can't, can't go!"

She felt herself flushing under Tarquin's scrutiny. Then he led her to a chair and put her into it. "You are close to hysteria. Watch it," he warned. And then, "Brandy for that, I think," he said, and went to fetch it.

He said, "If you've made up your mind, we can have Bridgeman paged at the airport. I'll see to it. In his place, I doubt if I'd 'understand', but – ". He shrugged and, watching her drink in sips, added, "What is it about potential disaster for Eirene that seems to destroy all your self-possession, I wonder? I remember a time once before when – "

She stared down into the amber liquid. "Because it was the same then as it is now – you had made me responsible for her, and I failed her then, as I have now," she muttered thickly.

"*That* time, by losing touch with her for an hour? Oh, come!" he urged.

"This time it was more than that. Worse," she insisted.

"More? Worse? And 'responsible' – you? There was nothing you could have done to prevent the accident. Either

172

Eirene lost her nerve or her brakes failed – we may never know which, unless she can tell us. The wretched machine, the police say, was a write-off – "

But Clare's panic fears had caught at a word. She put aside the glass and looked up, her eyes wide. "Unless?" she echoed. "You think Eirene – may not . . . may not – ?"

"Nonsense. I meant until," he corrected quickly. "There's no question of critical danger for Eirene, none at all. And you have nothing with which to blame yourself either. I didn't depute you to police the child every hour of every day, and as I understand it, you weren't even there until just before she took that turn on to the Via Spoleto."

"But I told you!" Clare protested, her voice shrill. "I *told* you I signalled her to do it!"

He nodded. "Yes, so you said. And – ?"

"Well" – blankly – "that's all. *I* made her take the turn, and I should have known she couldn't do it. I remember thinking that she mustn't continue at that speed down the next steep bit, and that the uphill of Spoleto should stop her. But I was wrong, and when I saw the awful juddering of her handle-bars as she crashed, I realised that my trying to be clever might have k-killed her; that – that it was all my fault . . . all mine!'

Clare's last words came through teeth that chattered. She knew she was giving way to frenzy; knew Tarquin must despise her for it; knew she must, *must* control the weak tears of guilt and self-pity which welled in her eyes – and suddenly found Tarquin on his knees before her, his arms around her body, his troubled face level with hers. And to her infinite wonder he was comforting her, not despising her; being kind, and more than kind – saying loving things, using man-to-woman loving words, calling her "Clare darling" and "*Carissima mia*", mixing English and Italian in turn.

She looked at him through misty eyes, then rubbed them

clear with the backs of her fingers. "Don't," she murmured. "Don't, please, say things you don't mean, for – for sympathy's sake. I was wretched, and I did want you to understand – as sometimes you do, though not always. But I'm all right now, and you don't have to pretend – I can't bear it – from you, of all people."

"And why not from me, 'of all people'?"

"Because – " Self-preservation warned her not to say it, but in this emotionally charged atmosphere she did. "Because, from you, it hurts too much," she told him.

"*Hurts*! And supposing I wasn't pretending? Would all that I said in love and pity for you hurt too much, then?"

"In – love?" She shook her head. "You don't mean that. Not for me."

"You don't want me to mean it? Clare, look at me – " His finger and thumb were firm upon her chin. "Why do you think I insisted on a final talk with you before you left San Marino – and me – for good?"

"I – I don't know."

"Then listen now. I couldn't know then that any such strained circumstances as today's would break down the barrier between us. I thought we should part in coolness, but it was a final throw which I argued I owed myself – to tell you, before I let you go and before you went irrevocably into Oscar Bridgeman's arms, that I loved you too . . . wanted you, though accepting that you didn't want me. I had done what I could to ease the way for you both, but I intended you should know all you had come to mean to me while you have been here."

"You believed that Oscar and I –? You thought I was in love with him?"

"Have you ever told me differently?"

"I've never told you more than that we are friends."

"You were on outwardly loving terms."

174

Clare remembered. "Because you saw me kiss him once? That was on impulse – a kind of thank-you for a friendship that didn't ask more than I could give. And I don't understand – What had you done to make things easy for us? You wouldn't help Oscar with advice when I asked you to."

"And risked – and earned – your misjudgment of me by ensuring, in the only way I could, that he went back to England – where you'd be going too – with enough money in his pocket to guarantee you the kind of start to marriage which I wanted *you* at least to have. I made conditions to my buying of his land – remember?"

Clare said wonderingly, "And I thought –!"

Tarquin smiled faintly. "At the time you made it painfully clear *what* you thought, *cara mia*!"

"But really you did all that – for me?"

"For love of you. I had no other way of showing you it."

She looked away, shy of him. "If it's true, you could have told me so before now."

"When it is only now – today, under stress, that you have allowed me to know I had the power to hurt you?"

"You've had that for a long time."

"Since when? Tell me?"

"Always, I think. At first, you could hurt just my pride. I hated to fail you. But afterwards . . . since –"

He waited, then encouraged her, "Since? Come, my Clare, if you are telling me that I've been able to hurt you through love, you must say it in so many words sooner or later. Come – if I dare hope you mean it – 'I love you too, Tarquin' – Say it after me, and the wonder and the magic can begin from there –"

Bewildered, but willingly, happily, she said it, or had begun to, when the telephone rang, intruding, breaking the spell, bringing them back to the harsh realities of the day.

Clare breathed, "Eirene –!" and Tarquin stood, releasing

175

her. "Yes," he said gravely, and went to the telephone. "*Pronto?*"

Clare listened, heard his non-committal, "Yes" and again "Yes" and then "At once, of course" and after that, other things, the drift of which she did not grasp. At last he replaced the receiver and turned to her, his arms wide, ready to encircle her as she ran blindly into them, fearing to hear the worst.

He stroked her hair. "Stop trembling," he said. "It wasn't the hospital. It was Eirene's parents. They are at the airport, and they've come – together – to take her home."

CHAPTER TEN

Now this strange day had reached its evening. The sun had gone down in a splendour of red and gold cloud – the signal for San Marino to don its own encircling necklaces of lights and for its streets and squares to empty and quieten as people went home to their evening meal before meeting again for the nightly drink and gossip in the cafés.

After its overcharged hours, the Casa was also at pause now, its bad news faced, its good news shared and enjoyed, its surprises absorbed, though for her part Clare wondered if she would ever get used to the idea of Tarquin's loving her, of needing her to love him.

So far, anyway, she had had so little time! For upon that totally unexpected summons to him to meet Eirene's parents at the airport, he and Clare had had to shelve their sweet discovery of each other when he took her with him to the Casa to break the news of Eirene's accident to the Signora and to tell her of the Landors' arrival together at Rimini.

Shocked and worried as she clearly was about Eirene, Emilia Roscuro's reaction was characteristically controlled, and she earned all Clare's gratitude for her understanding of the choice for which Clare still blamed herself.

"Nonsense, child," the Signora ruled. "You did the right

thing as you saw it; no one can do more. And if Eirene hadn't agreed she should do as you advised, she would not have obeyed you, and still might have been wrong – who knows?"

But Clare, doubting that Eirene's panic had been capable of anything but blind obedience to her disastrous signal, had taken no comfort for her guilt until Tarquin had suddenly questioned, "It was noon, you say?" and had recalled aloud that at that hour the children from St. Agnese's Convent lower down the hill would be milling out from morning school ... Upon which his mother had commented quietly, "You see, child – from all which you may have saved Eirene and those babes?" and Clare, visualising Eirene's rogue machine hurtling down, ploughing in amongst them, felt blessedly absolved. Fate had been very kind.

Tarquin had had to leave for the airport then, but not before Nurse Lorenz had allowed him a glimpse of his newborn nephew, though not of Nicola who was asleep. He had remembered too to arrange for Oscar to be paged and asked Clare if she wanted him told to ring her when the message reached him. She had said Yes.

"What are you going to tell him?" Tarquin asked.

"Why, about Eirene; why I couldn't see him off."

"And the rest?"

She blushed. "The – rest?"

He had laughed, had tilted her chin and kissed her lightly on the lips. "Very well. Just tell him that you won't be following him to England just yet –" But there again the telephone had intruded and, on the point of leaving, he had stayed to answer it.

This time it was the hospital on the line. Eirene had now had a thorough X-ray. There were no internal injuries; she had almost completely recovered from shock, and her surgeon agreed that her parents could certainly see her when they arrived. And so Tarquin had finally departed, leaving Clare to tell his mother that he would brief and prepare the Landors before taking them to the hospital, where he might leave them to be alone with Eirene and return for them later.

His final promise to Clare had been, "*We'll* make it alone together some time, my love, even if it has to be after dark on the top of the Cesta Tower!" Then he was really gone.

There had followed an unusual, disjointed afternoon, with no withdrawn hour of siesta for anyone. For Clare it was a time of secret dreams and questionings which she had to keep to herself; for the rest of Tarquin's family it was one of speculation and plans and thinkings-aloud and frequent reassurances to each other that all must now go well with Eirene and that the significance of the surprise descent of her parents upon her and San Marino must surely mean that they had solved their differences and the three would be united again.

The Signora said so to Clare more than once and, efficiently taking over the reins of domestic management from Nicola, summoned Anna to a parley on the hospitality and accommodation to be accorded to her niece and her husband when they came and would be staying.

That night's dinner and tomorrow's luncheon menus were discussed; when Eirene was allowed home she must have a more convenient room than the tower room; the Landors must have the blue suite tonight. Anna would see that it was ready, please? Anna would, and had bustled off happily, her deflated sense of importance and superiority to Nurse Lorenz fully restored. Monthly nurses had had their little hour once the baby was born; respected housekeepers went on for ever, said Anna's eloquent back view as she returned to her own quarters.

Oscar had rung up and Clare, answering the telephone, dreaded his disappointed reaction to her broken promise to see him off. But Tarquin's message had been delayed by the

179

information desk, and when Oscar had heard it and was answering it, his flight number had already been called. There had been time enough only for Clare to tell him about the accident and to beg his understanding of why she hadn't turned up. And after his reassuring, "Not to worry. I'd watched and waited for you for so long that it's sheer relief to hear you on the line," he had had to go, sparing Clare from giving any hint of the news which, when he had to hear it, was going to be so difficult for her to tell.

Yet how could she have prepared him for it? she asked herself. By letting him guess her feeling for Tarquin? But how could that have helped, when she had believed there was no hope for her there? Oscar would have pitied her, sympathised, been kind. But it was too much to expect him not to try to persuade her she was wasting her spirit and would be wise to settle for second-best – the second-best of his own need of her. And supposing, in her despair of Tarquin, she had yielded to Oscar, that would have wronged them both. No, there was nothing, until today, that she could have said or done. And what, even now, did she know of her future? Except . . . except that Tarquin had told her he loved her! Beyond the wonder of that was a blank; a page of their story they hadn't yet written; a beginning of something so far without shape or plan. But a beginning. Surely?

In the late afternoon Nicola and the baby had held court. That is, Marco and Nicola held court in the name of the baby, who slept on, determinedly aloof from all personal remarks on his appearance, his admirable weight at birth, his alleged likeness to his family, and amiable discussion on what he should be called.

Stefano, perhaps? Or Giuseppe, after his grandfather? The name of Tarquin was mooted, but met a veto from the Signora, who said that Tarquin was, and always had been, the prerogative of Roscuro men. The discussion had been

180

shelved on Nicola's mild suggestion that perhaps she and Marco were the best judges of a name for their own child. All in good time before the christening Uncle Paolo should have it for entering on his chart.

Then Tarquin had returned, having left the Landors at the hospital. Before he took them there he said they had confided that all was well, and would be, between them now. Their six months' voluntary separation had proved to them both that to part for good would be unthinkable. For all their disputed ideas on its rights and duties, they had agreed that a marriage which had weathered twenty years could face the rest of a lifetime at not too much risk. By now it had gathered a valuable protective moss of associations and memories and family jokes and references which no one else could share, and it should grow more. They had both made concessions and yielded stubbornly-held positions, and they had decided on impulse to fly out to San Marino to tell Eirene so. Tarquin himself had seen Eirene briefly before leaving the three of them to their reunion, and had brought back a jaunty message from Eirene for Clare.

Tarquin reported, "She asked me to mention that the next time you saw fit to direct her to run her head against a stone wall, she would be greatly obliged if you could arrange to have it well padded." At which Clare found blessed relief in the laughter which everyone shared.

And now, as the swift darkness followed sunset, Tarquin had adroitly contrived a time and a place for Clare and himself to be alone together.

First, he had broken up the party at Nicola's bedside by telling his mother he had matters to discuss alone with her, and they had adjourned to her room. Returning after a while, he had persuaded Nurse Lorenz to allow Marco to stay with his wife until dinnertime. Both uncles had already disappeared of their own volition, and then the softly lighted *salotto*, with its door locked, became a lovers' meeting-place.

There was so much to say, to question, to answer, to promise, to explain, to discover! But at first mere words had to wait upon love expressed in touch and exploratory caress; in the clasp of arms; in the exchange of wry smiles at the surprise of it all; in the tenderness of lips upon lips and upon hair and eyelids and throat; and at last, upon a stronger tide which swept them along, in pliant surrender to fierce demand, both of them tossed into a maelstrom of desire which, in its turn, gradually quietened and set them free.

They were silent, only touching hands now, a little awed by the strength of the passion which their embrace had promised to each other. Fulfilment was for the future. But the promise had been there.

At last Clare stammered, "I – didn't know. You – you never let me guess!"

"Nor did you, *amante*!"

"But – when? How? Why?"

"Would you like me to tell you 'At first sight'?" he teased.

"No, because it couldn't be true. Your first sight of me was of a bedraggled rat on a high road!"

"Bedraggled, yes. Rat, no. But No also to 'first sight'. I think what first stirred my feeling for you was your courage in insisting that you should face your fiancé's family alone. That, and the spirit with which you defied 'family' to have any value for you or for any man who had the misfortune to fall in love with you; he having people of his own, people he would want you to accept. Family? Not for you, you said. Out of the frying-pan into the fire, you said. And that, I think, was when I hatched my plot to see more of you, to see what made you tick, as your slang has it."

"You pretended the job had been Nicola's idea!" she accused him. "And you couldn't have loved me for that tirade – you trounced me for it."

"I didn't say I loved you then. But you had intrigued me. You had got under my skin. It was only later that you became important, too important for my comfort – And what do you mean, that I didn't allow you to know? What about Christmas morning, when, to make an excuse to kiss you, I fed you with that nonsense about Befana?"

Clare remembered. "You mean it isn't true that she demands a forfeit? That is, of course it isn't *true*. But people don't even pretend it is?"

"Not a word of it. I saw my chance and made up a legend to fit on the spot. Oh, of course Befana punishes the bad children and rewards the good – we shall tell *our* children so – but she never thought up the one about breakable presents at risk. I did," Tarquin confessed.

"Tarquin, you – you wretch!"

"But I had been too clever. There was no response at all. I had demanded the forfeit, but you hadn't given it. I declare, you deserved to have that vase shatter into a thousand fragments before your very eyes!"

Clare laughed happily. "Instead it's my most treasured possession. And how could you expect me to respond, when you claimed it was only a kind of Christmas forfeit of a kiss?"

"Yet I hoped my – technique would tell you it was more than that."

She looked down shyly at their entwined hands. "I couldn't afford to believe your 'technique'," she said. "I had no idea you felt anything for me. And there was Jaquetta Fiore. I was jealous of her. And you were taking her about even after you claim now you had begun to love me."

"And must I explain Jaquetta?"

"Please –"

"Well, Jaquetta was there, on my scene, and Nicola's friend before you appeared. And though I've been a fairly contented

183

bachelor, I have my social side, and a man can't continually dine out or attend parties alone without being considered a freak. Hence Jaquetta. She was decorative enough for other men to envy me her company, and I never had to concoct excuses to kiss *her*. She made it all too easy."

"Then you did kiss her?" Clare pounced jealously.

Tarquin's lips brushed hers briefly. "In training for you," he murmured. "Besides, you were kissing Bridgeman, he claimed you openly as his 'girl', and one could tell from the way he looked at you – He filled your requirements for a man uncluttered by family too."

"But I told you I had regretted all that silly prejudice!" she protested. "That the closeness of your family had taught me better."

"Though in the next breath, claiming you must go back to England and forget us," he countered.

"Yes, well –"

"Yes, well –?" he mimicked. "And now supposing you tell what attraction you found in me?"

Clare hesitated. "At first, your – sureness, I think," she said. "Your sureness of yourself, without a trace of conceit. Your authority; the way you expect a great deal of people and usually get it. And then – your kindness. And –" she stood back from him, surveying him. "And then it was you, just you – your looks, the way you walk, your voice – all of you! Don't make me analyse it, for it just isn't possible," she begged as she went into his arms again and hid her face in the hollow of his shoulder.

Presently she said, "I'm beginning to fear what your people may say – Nicola and her husband, and Eirene and your mother."

Tarquin said, "You ought to know that Nicola would wish nothing better for me, and that Eirene will be delighted. It will ultimately register with Uncles Paolo and Lucio that I am taking

184

a bride, whereupon Paolo will prepare to enter your name opposite to mine on the family tree, and Lucio will probably polish up a halberd or a breastplate as a christening present to our first son. And Mama isn't going to be surprised."

Clare looked up, startled. "She must be! She can't have expected – And Nicola told me she thought you would marry Jaquetta."

"She doesn't now. Since Giorgio Fiore's disgrace and their cowardly flight, goodness knows where, Jaquetta has been in the past tense for Mama. And as she knows now about you and me, you haven't to fear her surprise, my darling."

"She knows about us? But how can she?"

"Because," Tarquin said simply, "I've just told her. Before I brought you here, and Mama would regard it as slightly *brutta figura* to betray surprise at an accomplished fact."

Clare shook her head at him. "How you exaggerate! She must have said *something* to show what she thought."

"She did. She congratulated me. Said you were a daughter she could learn to love, and that it was high time a Roscuro married outside his race, since it was more than a century since one did. What's more," he added, "by the time I take you to her quite soon, I shouldn't be surprised if she hasn't already begun on plans to move into the villa, and to make it over to her own taste." He paused. "Because you know that is what will happen, don't you, *cara mia*? When we marry, you will be mistress here; Nicola will stay until she is next able to join Marco wherever he is stationed, and Uncle Paolo and Uncle Lucio will still make it their home?"

Clare nodded. "Yes, of course. It is I who will be the interloper."

"*Interloper?* As my *wife*? You will be a Roscuro – one of our people! But you accept the conditions of marrying me – the family commitments and the loyalties you will take on and share – the smoke into the flame?"

185

She smiled. "There are families – and families," she reminded him.

"And men – and men?"

"For me – one man," she said.

A GREAT IDEA!

We have chosen some of the works of Harlequin's world-famous authors and reprinted them in the 3 in 1 Omnibus. Three great romances — COMPLETE AND UNABRIDGED — by the same author — in one deluxe paperback volume.

Joyce Dingwell (2)

The Timber Man (#917)
It was bad enough to have to leave Big Timbers, but even worse that Blaze Barlow should think Mim was leaving for the wrong reasons.

Project Sweetheart (#964)
Alice liked being treated as though she were something special—she privately believed she was. Then Bark Walsh, the project boss, suddenly ended her reign!

Greenfingers Farm (#999)
It never occurred to Susan that circumstances were not as they seemed, and that her well-intentioned efforts as companion, were producing the wrong results!

Mary Burchell (2)

Take Me With You (#956)
Lucy fought hard for a home of her own—but it was her return to the old orphanage that provided the means to achieve it.

The Heart Cannot Forget (#1003)
Andrea didn't take Aunt Harriet seriously about inheriting her estate until she met her aunt's dispossessed and furious nephew Giles and his even angrier fiancee.

Choose Which You Will (#1029)
As companion to old Mrs. Mayhew, Harriet expected a quiet country life—but quickly found her own happiness at stake in a dramatic family crisis.

Elizabeth Hoy

Snare The Wild Heart (#992)
Eileen had resented Derry's intrusion to make a film of the island, but she realized now that times had changed and Inishbawn must change too!

The Faithless One (#1104)
Brian had called her love an interlude of springtime madness but Molly knew that her love for him would never quite be forgotten.

Be More Than Dreams (#1286)
Anne suddenly realized her love for Garth was more important that anything else in the world—but how could she overcome the barrier between them.

Roumelia Lane

House Of The Winds (#1262)
Laurie tricked Ryan Holt into taking her on safari despite his "no women" rule—but found it was only the first round she'd won!

A Summer To Love (#1290)
"A summer to love, a winter to get over it," Mark had once joked. But Stacey knew no winter would help her get over Mark.

Sea Of Zanj (#1338)
A change of scenery, a little sun, a chance for adventure—that's what Lee hoped for. Her new job didn't work out quite that way!

LOOK WHAT YOU MAY BE MISSING

Listed below are the 26 Great Omnibus currently available through **HARLEQUIN READER SERVICE**

Essie Summers #1
Bride In Flight (#933)
Meet on My Ground (#1326)
Postscript To Yesterday (#1119)

Jean S. MacLeod
The Wolf of Heimra (#990)
Summer Island (#1314)
Slave Of The Wind (#1339)

Eleanor Farnes
The Red Cliffs (#1335)
The Flight Of The Swan (#1280)
Sister Of The Housemaster (#975)

Isobel Chace
A Handful Of Silver (#1306)
The Saffron Sky (#1250)
The Damask Rose (#1334)

Joyce Dingwell #1
The Feel Of Silk (#1342)
A Taste For Love (#1229)
Will You Surrender (#1179)

Sara Seale
Queen of Hearts (#1324)
Penny Plain (#1197)
Green Girl (#1045)

Mary Burchell #1
A Home For Joy (#1330)
Ward Of Lucifer (#1165)
The Broken Wing (#1100)

Susan Barrie
Marry A Stranger (#1034)
The Marriage Wheel (#1311)
Rose In The Bud (#1168)

Violet Winspear #1
Palace of Peacocks (#1318)
Beloved Tyrant (#1032)
Court of the Veils (#1267)

Jane Arbor
A Girl Named Smith (#1000)
Kingfisher Tide (#950)
The Cypress Garden (#1336)

Anne Weale
The Sea Waif (#1123)
The Feast Of Sara (#1007)
Doctor In Malaya (#914)

Essie Summers #2
His Serene Miss Smith (#1093)
The Master of Tawhai (#910)
A Place Called Paradise (#1156)

Catherine Airlie
Doctor Overboard (#979)
Nobody's Child (#1258)
A Wind Sighing (#1328)

Violet Winspear #2
Bride's Dilemma (#1008)
Tender Is The Tyrant (#1208)
The Dangerous Delight (#1344)

Rosalind Brett
The Girl at White Drift (#1101)
Winds of Enchantment (#1176)
Brittle Bondage (#1319)

Kathryn Blair
Doctor Westland (#954)
Battle of Love (#1038)
Flowering Wilderness (#1148)

Iris Danbury
Rendezvous In Lisbon (#1178)
Doctor at Villa Ronda (#1257)
Hotel Belvedere (#1331)

Mary Burchell #2
Take Me With You (#956)
The Heart Cannot Forget (#1003)
Choose Which You Will (#1029)

Amanda Doyle
A Change for Clancy (#1085)
Play The Tune Softly (#1116)
A Mist In Glen Torran (#1308)

Rose Burghley
Man of Destiny (#960)
The Sweet Surrender (#1023)
The Bay of Moonlight (#1245)

Joyce Dingwell #2
The Timber Man (#917)
Project Sweetheart (#964)
Greenfingers Farm (#999)

Roumelia Lane
House of the Winds (#1262)
A Summer to Love (#1280)
Sea of Zanj (#1338)

Margaret Malcolm
The Master of Normanhurst (#1028)
The Man In Homespun (#1140)
Meadowsweet (#1164)

Elizabeth Hoy
Snare the Wild Heart (#992)
The Faithless One (#1104)
Be More Than Dreams (#1286)

Anne Durham
New Doctor at Northmoor (#1242)
Nurse Sally's Last Chance (#1281)
Mann of the Medical Wing (#1313)

Marjorie Norell
Nurse Madeline of Eden Grove (#962)
Thank You, Nurse Conway (#1097)
The Marriage of Doctor Royle (#1177)

The books outlined throughout these pages are but a few of the many romantic novels available through Harlequin Reader Service. We hope you will find them appealing, and if so, please refer to the coupon below for ordering instructions. We'll be happy to forward complete catalogue listings, detailed information and your copy of LUCIFER'S ANGEL by Violet Winspear, if you fill in and send us the coupon on the previous page.